471

FOOL'S PARADISE

In a fit of pique, Milly Morton — confidential 'secretary' to industrialist Mortimer Bland — deliberately smashed the astronomical plates of Bland's Chief Scientist, Anton Drew. Furthermore, she'd destroyed data which would warn the world of a forthcoming cosmic disaster. The unprecedented violent storms, signs of approaching doom, went unrecognized. Eventually Drew, aided by his friends Ken and Thayleen West, convinced the Prime Minister of the danger — but would it be too late to save the world?

JOHN RUSSELL FEARN

FOOL'S PARADISE

Complete and Unabridged

LINFORD
Leicester

First published in Great Britain

First Linford Edition
published 2009

British Library CIP Data

Fearn, John Russell, *1908 – 1960*
    Fool's paradise.—Large print ed.—
Linford mystery library
1. Suspense fiction
2. Large type books
I. Title
823.9′12 [F]

ISBN 978–1–84782–567–4

Published by
F. A. Thorpe (Publishing)
Anstey, Leicestershire

Set by Words & Graphics Ltd.
Anstey, Leicestershire
Printed and bound in Great Britain by
T. J. International Ltd., Padstow, Cornwall

This book is printed on acid-free paper

Acknowledgements

From the theory briefly expressed in Chapter 1, acknowledgements are due to Lyle Gunn's article 'The Magnetic Field'.

1

Thayleen West lowered her slender white hands from the piano keyboard and smiled to herself. She was satisfied with her music, herself, and her home. She had world fame as a concert pianist, and she had Kenyon, her husband —

She turned as he entered the room. It was late afternoon. The room was full of golden hues and soft, blurry shadows. Outside, through the french windows, the well kept garden drooped in saturating August heat.

'That was wonderful, Thay!' Kenyon came hurrying forward and caught the girl's hands in his own. He was a lanky, genial soul, an engineer and a materialist, yet it did not make him an intolerable husband. Materialism and artistry could — and did — go hand-in-hand.

'A change for us to be together,' Ken continued, putting an arm round the girl's shoulders. 'If only all Sundays were like this!'

'They will be, after this year,' Thayleen said.

Ken smiled to himself and strolled to the open windows. He gazed out on the sunlight. His keen grey eyes followed the flight of a bird as it cavorted gaily in sombre blue heaven.

'You said that last year, Thay,' he reminded her. 'And the year before that. By all means go on playing to the world, but — sometimes — '

Thayleen rose. She was only five feet tall, slender as a willow. With wraith-like silence she crossed to where her husband stood. Her dark head with its piled-up curls just reached his shoulder.

'Sometimes — what?' she questioned.

'Nothing, dear. Just thinking . . . '

Ken smiled down on her good-humouredly. His boyish appearance, which his tousled blond hair and plain good-natured face did little to belie, had no relationship to his mind. Machines — buildings — bridges — liners — power-houses — jet planes. He was always thinking about them, or else Thayleen — or the future.

'Nothing?' Thayleen repeated, surprised.

'Well, I'm wondering where we're going to finish up.'

'What a thought!' Thayleen laughed.

'A serious one, though. We've been married two years and seen each other about five times. You're in New York, London, Paris, all over the place. I make love to your televised image, I listen to you over the radio. It's like having a synthetic wife!'

'Not altogether,' Thayleen said quietly. 'A synthetic wife couldn't — couldn't add one more to the family, could she?'

Ken did not immediately grasp the point. When he did he swung round to meet Thayleen's dark eyes with the sunlight glancing through them.

'Thay — you mean — ?' He stopped and gripped her arms.

'Yes. In the autumn. Four more concerts and then I'll retire to attend to other things.'

'Lord!' Ken looked confused. 'Have

— you told anybody else?'

'Not yet.'

'Then I'm going to. Particularly Anton.'

Thayleen gave a serious glance. 'And be rewarded with the observation that a biological function is about to take place? Ken, dear, why waste your time? Anton's a brilliant chap, I know, but so utterly cold-blooded.'

'Only because he's a scientist. I've got to tell him!'

'As you will,' Thayleen shrugged.

Ken lost himself in speculations for a moment. Thayleen glanced up as the sun became veiled by a passing cloud. It was surprising how dark it seemed to make the countryside, which for many weeks had been drenched in pitiless heat. Strange, too, for the British Isles, which had usually managed to ruin its summer with rain. Now everybody was crying out for it. Prayers in the churches, cattle nosing into iron-hard waterholes; crops yellow before their time; farmers rubbing the backs of their leathery necks and gazing up into a brazen vault from which all moisture seemed to have evaporated. It

4

seemed that throughout the Western hemisphere one vast anticyclone existed. The summer had, so far, been the hottest in history.

Not that Kenyon West minded. He was not thinking of the present, but of the future — of the son or daughter yet to come.

The cloud passed. The sunlight flooded down on the world again. At the far end of the garden the trees wilted, aching, as though they found it beyond them to stand up straight in the bone dry soil . . .

★   ★   ★

On the following day, the commencement of a new week, Thayleen departed for the Continent and a further round of concert tours. Ken for his part was thankful for a mountain of work to keep his mind occupied. As Chief Engineer of the immense Mid-England Steel and Iron Combine he had plenty to do. Upon him, at the moment, rested the responsibility for the cutting of a subsidiary bore to the existing Channel Tunnel, making it possible for more traffic to be handled to and from the Continent.

Even so he took the opportunity one evening to visit Anton Drew, his friend from college days and now the head of Bland's Enterprises — which controlled the output of all the world's rare drugs, medicines, chemicals, and atomic and plastic by-products.

Ken first tried Drew's Surbiton apartment and then realised he should have had more sense. Drew was a bachelor who spent every waking hour at some scientific pursuit or other — and there was no better place for this than the replete scientific laboratories where he worked. Outside interests never attracted him in the least.

Sure enough, Ken found him in the remoter parts of the Bland laboratories, to which quarter he was directed by a night watchman, the normal staff having long since departed. Their interest in things scientific always evaporated at six o'clock.

Not so Anton Drew. He regarded scientific pursuits as a mother does the development of her child. More often than not he even forgot to collect his salary cheque: even more often did he forget he needed a clean overall.

When Ken came upon him he was in the big solar observatory maintained by Bland Enterprises for the sole purpose of manufacturing solar scale maps for the world's observatories, and cross-checking much astronomical data. In a word, the commercial genius of Mortimer Bland had turned science to account in the matter of money. He held the rights on nearly every scientific product, but it was the brains of Anton Drew that made the whole complicated scheme workable.

'So here you are!' Ken exclaimed cordially, advancing with hand extended.

Anton Drew did not answer. He was seated at a desk near the giant reflector, busy studying a sheet of figures. A short briar crackled in his mouth; his untidy brown hair was flung back in confusion from his wide forehead. With a smile Ken noticed that the collar of the scientist's overall was half up and half down. For the rest he could only see the slim, wiry shoulders, hooked nose, jutting chin, and unusually large mouth.

Then Drew looked up and after gazing absently with pale blue eyes for nearly thirty seconds he seemed to awaken.

'Hello,' he greeted, and remained thoughtful.

Ken sat down, not in the least offended. That three weeks had passed since he had last seen Drew did not signify. Drew always talked as though there had been no gap in conversation.

'Busy?' Ken ventured.

'Eh? Oh, busy? Yes, of course I'm busy!' Drew brooded, allowed his pipe to go out, then brooded again. 'Very busy,' he resumed at last. 'It's this unusual weather.'

'Unusual — but glorious,' Ken smiled.

'Calm before the storm,' Drew muttered, and got to his feet.

He was only small, spare as a youth, certainly not looking his forty-eight years.

'You mean thunder?' Ken asked, puzzled. 'Well, I suppose it will break up in that. So what?'

Drew gave an odd glance, somehow

8

mystifying. He made another effort to light his pipe. Propping himself against the massive eyepiece of the reflector he scowled pensively.

'I thought you'd like to know, Anton, that Thayleen's expecting a youngster in the autumn,' Ken hurried on. 'I've been holding it back. Bit of a surprise, eh?'

Drew gazed into the distance. 'It must be the beginning of the hundred-year-cycle,' he said.

'What is?' Ken looked blank. 'Dammit, man, listen! I said Thayleen is expecting a baby.'

'She is?' Drew smiled briefly. 'Good! Fine! Normal enough for a married couple, isn't it? Simple biological function — Er, where was I?'

'At the beginning of a hundred-year cycle,' Ken answered sourly. 'And thanks for the congratulations!'

Drew came to life for a moment. With an apologetic grin he lounged forward.

'Sorry, old man — really I am.' He clapped Ken on the shoulder. 'I've been so absorbed in this sunspot business I haven't been able to think of much else.

9

Of course I congratulate you, and Thayleen too. Don't spoil the brat . . . '

He sucked at his pipe and continued, 'This weather has something to do with sunspots. I don't quite know what. It is rather like a man who is about to die suddenly finding himself healthier than he has ever been before. Just as though Earth, about to die, is enjoying all the calmness preceding the hell to come.'

'What *are* you rambling about?' Ken demanded. Drew turned to the desk and raised six photographic plates. He handed them over and, as he looked at them Ken recognised spectro-heliograph records of the sun.

'That's what I'm talking about,' Drew said. 'Study them.'

'Mmmm — sunspots,' Ken said finally. 'About a dozen of them, big and small. How far does that get us?'

'They are getting bigger,' Drew said. 'If you'll look carefully you'll find the first plates were taken eight weeks ago. There are six plates there, taken at different times. First we see two spots — one big and one small. Then, as the weeks progress, they become more numerous; until on this last plate you will find them splotching away from the solar equator down towards its poles. That has never happened before in the sun's history.'

'I'm a bit hazy about this,' Ken said, 'but shouldn't an outburst of spots like this cause magnetic storms?'

'It should, but we don't happen to have had any in our part of the world. Sunspots are queer phenomena. Sometimes they violently upset the weather conditions and electrical equipment; at other times they create anticyclone conditions, and calm, burning weather such as we have been experiencing lately. What is somewhat terrifying — to me anyway — is that we are at one start of a hundred-year-period of sunspots. This sunspot spread may continue indefinitely.'

Ken ventured a suggestion. 'With a consequent dimming of the sun, due to so much of his face being caverned with spots? Is that it?'

Drew took the plates back and relit his pipe.

'There will be a decrease in light, yes,

but that isn't what is worrying me. It is the appalling danger to Earth's magnetic field! The Earth is a magnet, you know, and like any other magnet is surrounded by a magnetic field. If you want proof of it look at the compass needle revealing the lines of force between the two poles.'

'High school stuff,' Ken said. 'What about it?'

'That magnetic field, Ken, is our protection against appalling disaster! If it were to break down the consequences would be terrible, and it is because the possibility exists that I am so worried. As yet I cannot seem to get all the astronomers to worry with me, but they will as the spots multiply. The more the sunspots increase, the greater becomes the danger of the magnetic field collapsing.'

Ken gave a half smile, and then it faded. Knowing Drew as he did, knowing his profound scientific knowledge and that he only concerned himself with facts, it was disturbing to find him so uneasy. He never worried without good reason.

'Sunspots go in cycles,' Drew explained.

'Highs and lows return in approximately eleven years — but there are other variations in their regularity which are the outcome of another independent cycle of more than a century's duration. Up to now, the high of the eleven-year and the hundred-year cycles have never matched, though astronomers have known for long enough it must do so in about a year hence. It means the absolute maximum of sunspot activity, an activity never known in the history of the world. With those high cycles working together, and at maximum, our magnetic field might collapse!'

Ken cast a glance towards the window. There was a rectangle of evening sky with a star gleaming between the sides of lofty buildings. The extraordinary peace made it hard for him to believe . . .

'Frankly, Anton,' he said, after a moment, 'I'm hazy about what the magnetic field does. I'm an engineer not an astronomer.'

'The magnetic field,' Drew said, 'is our only protection against cosmic rays. It is so strong that only cosmic rays of energy greater than 200-million electron volts can penetrate it, but when these do penetrate things happen. You find two-headed chickens, double-fingered children, five-legged calves — all kinds of monstrosities. Why? Because the parental germ-plasm has been accidentally struck by cosmic radiation which has completely distorted it, with the result that a freak is born . . . '

Drew took his pipe from his teeth and contemplated it.

'Under present conditions, Ken, with the magnetic field doing its normal job, the chances of a hit by cosmic rays are infinitely remote, but the cases I have instanced show it does happen every now and again. Roughly speaking, the cosmic rays aim thirty shots at every living body every second, and each body has something like a thousand trillion trillion atoms. But consider these atoms, as apart as island universes, each with their planetary electrons separated from the nucleus by distances proportionate to those between members of the Solar System — Then we see why a direct hit is unlikely. The cosmic radiation projectiles, as we might call them, go straight through empty space.

'Consider, though, the effect if the field were only partially weakened. Eight hundred million billion cosmic rays strike Earth every second with a thousand times the voltage of lightning. Imagine even a part of that inconceivable energy raining down upon us, upon everything. Life as we would know it would cease. The most incredible changes would occur. It would be . . . the end of the world.'

'Not very cheering,' Ken muttered, 'but I don't see the connection between the magnetic field and sunspots, though. How do they affect each other?'

'The atomic storms of the sun — sunspots — are responsible for its own magnetic field,' Drew answered. 'The stronger the solar field becomes, the weaker becomes the Earth's. That is elementary law. Hence, a vast number of sunspots will enormously increase the sun's potential and correspondingly lower Earth's field. We may survive this hundred-year-cycle of spots with nothing worse than violent magnetic storms, which are bound to develop before long;

15

or we may have something much worse to contend with if the spots continue to increase.'

Ken got to his feet.

'How long have you known of this possibility?' he asked.

'Does it signify?'

'Of course it does! Isn't it time the authorities were told about it?'

'No use,' Drew answered, shrugging. 'Even most of the astronomers think I'm a scaremonger, so you can imagine the reaction of the Government!'

'I can't see why reputable astronomers refuse to listen to you.'

'I'll tell you why.' Drew's face became grim. 'They just haven't the imagination to hurdle the gap between the obvious and the possible. Astronomy, to them, is just routine. They fail to realise that these sunspots, unchecked, might cause catastrophe. In any case, if the Governments of the world were told think of the panic! The population of Earth would look like an overturned anthill.'

'I suppose,' Ken said, after a troubled interval, 'it is rather foolish to plan for the

16

future? As things are?'

'I suppose it is,' Drew agreed, musing. Silence.

'Well, I don't believe it!' Ken declared at last. 'It isn't that I doubt you: it's just that I can't credit the human race being blotted out. Look at the things we have achieved. Destruction would just knock the bottom out of all reason for living!'

'I take a dim view of humanity myself,' Drew sighed. 'Here we are in the 21st century, still so absorbed in thinking up ways of killing each other we still haven't mastered some of the more virulent diseases, or how to properly feed everyone on the planet. To my mind, humanity deserves to be blotted out.'

'Anton — do you think I should tell Thayleen of your theory?'

'Why worry the poor girl?' Drew gave a shrug. 'If she thinks the world is coming to an end her musical gifts may go to pot. Why bother upsetting her? She'll know soon enough when the news can't be suppressed any more.'

Ken gave an uneasy smile. 'I came here to tell you I expect to be a father, and you hand me the end of the world! We certainly cover the ground, don't we?'

'Yes. Like you, there is much I wanted to do.'

'Wanted?' Ken repeated. 'That sounds as though you regard the end as inevitable, and not just a possibility.'

'I have been trying to let you down lightly,' Drew admitted quietly. 'Perhaps that wasn't very sensible, since you are anything but a weakling. Beyond a shadow of doubt, Ken, the end of the world *is* coming because it is scientifically impossible to escape it.'

'But you hinted at a doubt — !'

'I'd have let you go away thinking that, only my past tense a moment ago tripped me up. Listen, Ken, the naked facts are these: Sunspots are constantly increasing, and we are only at the start of a hundred-year-cycle in which is incorporated the normal eleven-year cycle. The spots cannot possibly get less for the next hundred years! A *century*, man! Whether they will destroy the sun as they progress I don't know, though I imagine his collapse into a white dwarf is possible; but

18

long before that happens this world of ours will have become the target for the full blast of cosmic rays, and we ourselves will only be memories.'

'It sounds defeatist,' Ken said. 'There are plenty of brilliant scientists in the world, you amongst them. Knowing what is coming, can't something be done to avert it?'

'As far as I can see, no — though some worthwhile notions might emerge when all the scientists of the world get together to fight the problem. It seems to me that we are unprotected against naked cosmic power, and no science of our devising can master it. All we can do is try and protect ourselves, hang on to a battered shell of the world in the hope that we may survive.'

Ken was silent. For a long time he looked at the bench without seeing it.

'I shall not tell Thayleen,' he said at last.

'I shouldn't. Let her enjoy what's left of her life.'

'But not to be able to plan for the future! To know that one cannot see

19

beyond a few months — ! I just can't grasp it!'

'It takes time,' Drew admitted. 'But there it is.'

Ken did not afterwards remember shaking hands or saying goodbye. He came out into the calm summer evening and contemplated it. Deep down, he wondered if for once in his brilliant career Anton Drew had not made a mistake.

2

It was about the time that Ken left the Bland Edifice that Mortimer Bland himself was enjoying an agreeable evening amidst the soft lights and sweet music of the Heart Throb Café. It was situated in the centre of London's sprawling huddle of buildings — exclusively extravagant, hiding many a dubious *tête-à-tête*, its staff trained unswervingly to admit the fact that the customer is always right.

Mortimer Bland, one of the city's wealthiest industrialists, was a frequent visitor. So was Milly Morton, the unusually lovely blonde who invariably accompanied him. What Bland liked about Milly, apart from her curves, was the fact that his money could not only buy for her whatever she wished, but could also buy *from* her whatever *he* wished. Which to his commercial mind seemed a fair exchange.

They sat now in an alcove, their table

hidden — as were the other tables — from the rest of the café. The champagne was just right; so was the meal. Mortimer Bland was glowing like a well-fed bulldog and not looking unlike one, either. Money, hearty eating, and lack of exercise had given him a beefy face and bulgy grey eyes, but it had not yet greyed the black hair swept back from his forehead.

At sixty he was as strong as an ox, and proud of it. Milly was quite thirty-five years younger, but this fact did not bother her in the least when weighed against the advantages of being one of Bland's most favoured girl friends.

'I think,' Milly said, as she set down her champagne glass, 'that I'm going to ask you to do me a favour, Mort.'

Bland grinned and revealed yellow teeth. 'How much?'

Milly laughed, and it made her more beautiful. Bland liked her even white teeth and the way in which the concealed lighting caught the waves in her honey-coloured hair.

'It isn't money,' Milly said. 'I want a job.'

'What!' Bland stared at her. 'You, a musical comedy star, wanting a *job*?'

'My contract's run out, and nobody wants to renew it. I'm one of those girls who spend as they go and now I — Well, I have to stay alive, haven't I?'

Bland set his jaw. 'Nobody can kick you around like that, Milly! I'll get you into a new production if I have to buy up a chain of theatres to do it — '

'But I'm getting tired of the stage,' Milly interrupted. 'And it's time I planned for the future.'

'In what way?'

'I suppose we could get married, couldn't we? Or is that too prosaic? Besides, we wouldn't be such good friends if we married. I couldn't stand being your wife and shut up in that big house of yours.'

'Then we'll not even consider it,' Bland said, who had no intention of marrying his latest infatuation.

'So,' Milly said, smiling again, 'I'd like some kind of position in your organisation. There must be room for a little girl like me, surely?'

Bland never mixed business with pleasure. 'Afraid not, my dear. My business is scientific, and what do you know about science?'

'But surely everybody doesn't have to be a scientist, down to the office boy? What about the clerical side? I can't type or use a computer but I'd soon learn.'

Bland poured out more champagne whilst he considered; then he asked a question, 'Why this decision to get into my organisation?'

Milly raised and lowered a semi-bare shoulder. 'Just the way it is. I'd feel safer with you at the head of things.'

'You'd find me very different in business.'

'Not so different, Mort. You'd be nice to me. If you weren't, it might cause an awful lot of trouble.'

'In what way?'

'Well . . . ' Milly inspected her immaculate nails. 'We have had moments that wouldn't sound so good in print, haven't we? And you have written me letters. The dirt rakers are just waiting to throw mud at a famous personality like you, Mort.'

'Polite blackmail, eh?' Bland's steel-trap mouth set hard for a moment; then he relaxed. 'And how damned right you are! I don't blame you, Milly, because not being a saint myself I can see how you look at it. All right — what sort of a job do you want in my organisation?'

'Personal secretary.'

'Can't be done, my dear. Miss Hawkins has been with me for twenty-five years.'

'Then it's time she went. I've seen the old hag. I should think she frightens away more business than she brings.'

'She's indispensable,' Bland temporized.

'Nobody's that. Get rid of her.'

Milly finished her champagne and looked at Bland steadily with her sapphire blue eyes. Her smile had gone. Her red lips were set in a firm line. Her beautiful face was like marble.

'All right,' Bland said, shrugging. 'I'll manage something.'

'Good!' Milly smiled again. 'You see, Mort, our association works both ways. I've given you plenty up to now, and naturally there are other rewards I want besides the presents you give me. Not marriage or anything dull like that — just a comfortable job with a good salary of, say . . . ' she paused, and then named a high figure.

Bland jumped visibly. 'What!'

'To commence with,' Milly amended. 'A personal secretary has a lot of responsibility.'

'But it's preposterous! Miss Hawkins doesn't get anything like that.'

'Look at Miss Hawkins — then at me,' Milly suggested. 'I'll add glamour to the place.'

Bland was silent. His reputation must be kept undefiled at all costs: so much depended on it. He spent a few seconds cursing himself for a fool for not having been more careful in his lighter moments.

He knew he would have to agree. But later, perhaps he might think of a way round the problem. So he smiled at Milly genially, and she smiled back . . . but her blue eyes were as hard as the gems at her white throat.

★　★　★

26

The most surprised person at the institution of Milly as Bland's personal secretary was Anton Drew. The formidable Miss Hawkins had not been so much surprised as vitriolic, but had departed with the assurance that she could easily find a post with a rival concern.

For Milly, Drew's frozen contempt for her was something she could not tolerate, and one morning she said so to the great man himself.

'I want that creature fired!' she told Bland flatly, striding into his enormous office.

'Who? Oh, you mean the man who has just left? Drew?'

'Yes, Drew! That — that *thing* in the dirty overall who looks at me as though I'd crawled out of a drain.'

'He can't be fired,' Bland said calmly. 'He's the backbone of the organisation.'

'I know he's the chief scientist; he hasn't forgotten to tell me so — but any more looks like the one he gave me just now when he left and I'll blow up the place to get rid of him, if I have to!'

'Oh, for heaven's sake be reasonable!' Bland protested. 'I know he looks at everybody as if they don't count, but it's only his way. Don't antagonise him.'

Milly reflected, then her blue eyes gleamed.

'All right, maybe I can teach him manners . . .'

Ignoring Bland's protests as he struggled clumsily to rise from his swivel-chair, she hurried from the office, through her own secretarial sanctum, and out into the immaculate corridor which led to the major laboratory. When she had entered it she stood looking about her.

The gathered assistants, busy at their various tasks, looked long enough to wonder; then their eyes followed her lithe movements towards Drew's desk at the far end of the laboratory where he sat brooding over the latest spectro-heliograph plates.

'Listen, you!' Milly banged her fist on the desk.

Drew looked up, removing his pipe from his teeth,

'Well, Miss Morton?'

The cold level of his voice took her off balance.

'I think you and I should come to an understanding,' she continued. 'I don't like the way you behave towards me.'

'No?' Drew surveyed her and remarked she was an unusually lovely girl using an unusually lovely perfume.

'Next time,' Milly added, 'treat me as though I'm a human being and not one of those things that run up and down a jar.'

'You mean a culture? Cultures are interesting, Miss Morton.'

'Meaning I'm not?' Milly blazed. 'You confounded — '

'You are supposed to be a secretary,' Drew cut in. 'As such you are a supreme blunderer. You have beauty, Miss Morton, and everything that goes to make a young woman attractive — only I don't happen to be the type that can *be* attracted. I look only for efficiency in this organization, and I never get it from you. That is why I regard you as a confounded nuisance! In your own sphere I don't doubt that you are a great success: I'd be delighted if you'd return to it.'

Milly's highly rouged cheeks coloured more deeply — then in sudden uncontrollable rage she whipped up the spectroplates from the desk and slammed them with all her force to the floor. They splintered immediately on the hard rubberoid, shards of glass scattering in all directions.

Drew jumped to his feet, the whiteness of his face sufficient indication of his fury.

'You vicious, selfish little idiot!' he shouted. 'Do you realise what you've done? You've destroyed the very evidence upon which the saving of a world might depend — '

'World?' Milly repeated, half frightened, half stupid.

Drew came round the desk and clutched her arm fiercely.

In spite of all her protests he whirled down the corridor and into Mortimer Bland's office. Astounded, the big fellow sat staring.

'What the devil's all this about?' he demanded.

'You've an ultimatum on your hands, Mr. Bland,' Drew snapped. 'Either get rid of this playtime baby of yours, or I quit.'

'But what's happened?' Bland's prominent eyes popped.

Drew released the girl savagely and told of the laboratory incident.

'Those plates were beyond price,' he finished heatedly. 'Solar photographs which I'll need as proof of the — '

Drew stopped suddenly. Bland seized on the silence.

'Proof of what?' he demanded. 'And what the hell do you want spectro-plates for? They've nothing to do with this organisation, have they?'

'Only on the astronomical side, for the observatories.'

'No observatory has asked for spectro-plates, Drew. I see everything which goes out of this organisation. So what's the explanation?'

Drew pulled out his pipe and bit into it. 'Experimental work and very essential. Concerning the present rash of sunspots.'

Milly folded her rounded arms and gave Bland a glance.

'A man who can spend his time

studying sunspots doesn't seem so indispensable to me,' she remarked sourly. 'What have they got to do with the stuff this place turns out?'

'I could explain the whole thing, but the time isn't ripe for me to do so,' Drew retorted. 'All I can say now is that the destruction of those plates has ruined the work of months.'

Bland's eyes became hard. 'Listen to me, Drew. I engaged Miss Morton, and I stand by it; and I'm getting the impression that I've been mistaken in you, too. Your job is to supervise the science of this organisation, not study sunspots. I know we check astronomical findings with our observatory apparatus, but that doesn't mean you can make experiments on your own.'

'If it were not for the fact I'd start a panic, I'd tell you what it's all about!' Drew snapped.

'Nice of you! All I can see is that you have been using my time and instruments to your own advantage, besides insulting Miss Morton. There's only one answer to that.'

The shock-haired scientist hesitated, his cold eyes turning to consider Milly's triumphant face; then without a word he strode from the office and slammed the door behind him. Bland relaxed in his swivel chair with a sigh of relief.

'I wonder if we did right,' Milly mused.

'What?' Bland sat up again.

'I'm wondering about something he said,' Milly continued. 'Something about my destroying plates upon which the saving of a world depends. There was something rather *frightening* about the way he said it. Maybe he should have stayed on to work the thing out.'

'Which world?' Bland asked, puzzled.

'I don't know. I suppose he meant this one. What other world could there be?'

'Oh, there *are* others,' Bland assured her, none too certain of himself. 'Venus, Mars, and the rest of 'em in the System. But there's no reason why he should wish to save those, far as I can see.'

Silence. In the presence of Milly, Bland would not admit that Drew had left behind him a curious air of disquiet. Bland knew only too well that Drew was not the kind of man to keep silent about anything scientific unless it were vitally important that he do so — and somehow the saving of a world, and sunspots, had an unpleasant connection . . .

3

That evening Drew found his concentra-
tion in his town apartment interrupted by
the arrival of Ken West. The young
engineer looked vaguely surprised as he
followed Drew's untidy figure into the
small rear room he used as a private
laboratory. A single globe depending from
its flex cast a bright circle on the bench
where the scientist had been working.

'I went to the Bland Edifice,' Ken
explained, 'but the watchman told me
you'd left — for good.'

'Correct,' Drew agreed.

Ken sat down in sheer surprise. 'You
mean you quit?'

'Yes.' Drew returned to his stool and
sat there like a gnome, his eternal pipe
smouldering.

'But for why? You, of all people!'

'I left because of a woman — the
biggest bungling female ever turned loose
in a scientific organization. One of

Bland's spare tyres . . . ' and Drew added the details briefly

'That girl must sure be laughing,' Ken muttered.

'Let her — whilst she may. Nobody will laugh much before long, Ken. As for that girl's 'victory', I had either to tell Bland — who doesn't know the first thing about science — that the world is doomed, and thereby set everybody by the ears; or I had to keep quiet. I decided to keep quiet, or at least until plans can be worked out to control the panic which is bound to follow. Thanks to that girl's foolery my proof of sunspot progress is destroyed. That will make it doubly hard for me to convince the authorities.'

'But surely other observatories took similar plates?'

'Routine plates, yes: I've checked up on that during today, but not enough to build up the visual story I had worked out. I had no copies because I saw no reason for them. A scatterbrained fool like that Morton woman never occurred to me.'

'It's about the sunspot business that I came to see you. I still can't properly believe what you told me last night.'

'Then it's time you did,' the scientist replied. 'Now I have quit Bland's I haven't the apparatus for making studies of the solar disk, but Dick Hensley at Mount Wilson is a good friend of mine and he's giving me TV views and reports. The latest report shows the spots are still spreading, and a bolometer reading reveals a distinct drop in critical solar temperature. As temperature drops and spots enlarge Earth's magnetic field is correspondingly weakened. At the moment I am trying to calculate when we may expect real disaster.'

Ken glanced at the confusion of equations on the paper on the desk. Then he said, 'They have been having electrical storms in Paris, where Thayleen is playing. She 'phoned me about them today. They seem to have frightened her, too. Queer how we miss them, only across the Channel.'

Drew shrugged. 'Just chance. The storms follow electronic tracks and where they might travel nobody can predict. If they happen to drift this way we'll get a taste as well — but however violent the storms may be they will be footling compared to what will happen if the magnetic field gives way. In fact, Ken, I'd tell Thayleen to cancel her tour and leave Paris. Since it seems to be developing into a storm flashpoint there's no telling what may happen.'

'How am I to tell her that without giving the facts?'

'Think up an excuse. I'm just warning you: up to you how you work it out — Excuse me,' Drew broke off, as the visiphone shrilled for attention.

As Drew spoke a man's face appeared on the tiny screen.

'Glad I caught you, Mr. Drew. I'm Douglas Billington of the Agricultural Board. I tried to contact you at — '

'What's the trouble?' Drew interrupted.

'Hardly trouble. Rather joyous news as far as I am concerned, only I think an investigation should be made.'

'Of what?'

'The crops in Area 70 — and other

38

Areas as well — are unique! Cornstalks eight feet high, and barley bigger than that. It means a bumper harvest, but somehow it doesn't seem reasonable that the recent sunshine has caused such a bounty. So before cutting begins we'd like your opinion. Sometimes gargantuan growths are too rank for food.'

'Is there anything else unusual in growth?' Drew asked, thinking.

'Matter of fact, yes. In that particular area the grass is waist-high and the trees are growing far faster than normal.'

'Area 70 is in Surrey, is it not?' Drew asked, and the image in the scanning screen nodded. 'All right, I'll be over immediately. You'd better have floodlights put up for me.'

He switched off and began tugging at his overall. Ken watched him hurriedly scramble into a coat.

'What's so exciting?' Ken asked, having heard most of the conversation.

'This isn't a bounty; it may be the beginning of the end,' Drew answered. 'Care to come with me?'

'Nothing I'd like better.'

'Come on, then. My private helicar's on the roof.'

Drew whirled out of the apartment and led the way to the roof. Ten minutes later the little helicar was following a V-string of lights below and Drew looked into the distance where night-floods were beaming across the grain-growing land of Area 70. In another few minutes he had touched down and stepped out of the machine to find Douglas Billington and two of his Government colleagues waiting to greet him.

'Quick work,' Billington smiled, shaking hands. 'These two gentlemen represent the Farmers' Union.'

Drew nodded, shook hands, introduced Ken, and then said:

'Why did you pick on me for this job, Billington? Am I to work out of goodness of heart, or is it official?'

'Official. I reported the giant crops to the Government and they told me to get the best scientist to investigate. That meant you.'

'Thanks.' Drew gave his dry smile.

They began walking towards Billington's car.

'I hear you've left Bland?' Billington asked, puzzled.

'Difference of opinion. I'm freelancing.'

More than this Drew would not say. He settled in the car, his small figure wedged between those of the bigger men; then, as the vehicle began its journey from the airfield countryside, the criss-crossing beams of the night-floods became visible again, causing millions of candle-power brilliance across fantastic acres of motionless corn and barley.

'I never saw anything like that!' Ken exclaimed blankly.

Drew said nothing. He clambered out of the car and jammed the pipe in his teeth. Then he wandered with the rest of the men along the vista that had been cleared straight through the 'forest' of corn.

To Ken, the sense of unreality deepened as the walk progressed. Two feet overhead the enormous ears of corn were standing motionless in the windless air, etched sharply white against the night sky by the brilliance of the floods. The stalks of the corn were quite three inches across

41

and had the appearance of bamboo. From the base of the stems tough, stringy roots, apparently finding the soil surface not deep enough, had sprouted and dug hungry tendrils into the dust.

'Well?' Billington asked, as Drew halted. 'Queer, eh?'

Drew looked about him. 'Where's that waist-high grass you mentioned?'

'In the next Area — about a mile further on. I didn't have it floodlit, though.'

'Doesn't signify. I just want to look at it. Starlight should be sufficient.'

They went on again, their shoes cracking on the truncated stumps and roots where the agregious corn had been cut down. Ken, coming up in the rear, was suddenly reminded of the Biblical hordes passing through the divided Red Sea . . . Then they struck the rise of the land and came on its summit, to look down upon a sea of grass cloaking the side of a valley.

Here the wind was fresher. The moon, too, was rising, adding its pale light to that of the stars. The top of the grass weaved and flowed and contracted in a host of patterns, swinging great troughs of shadow across the area, troughs which were followed by flowing tides of silver light where in some oddly luminescent way the grass reflected the glow of stars and moon.

For a long time the men were silent, listening to the fairy rustling of the wilderness, their eyes following its eternally changing outline.

'Either my eyes are wrong, or else this confounded grass is reflective. I never noticed it before, but then I've never seen it at night. Only in the day. It has a look of the sea about it — the way breakers glitter as they fall on the shore.'

'Radioactivity,' Drew said obscurely, brooding.

'Can't be!' one of the officials protested. 'Whoever heard of radioactivity in pastures like these? They're purged free of all harmful ingredients.'

The scientist gave a taut grin in the moonlight, then looked down at his feet and stirred the parched dust with his shoe. The dust glittered momentarily like powdered diamonds.

'Give me an old envelope, somebody,' he requested, going down on one knee.

Ken found one in his wallet, and handed it over. Drew scraped some of the soil into it, taking care to use the edge of his shoe and not his bare hands. Then he stood up again.

'I haven't made an analysis yet, of course,' he said, 'but even without it I can tell you that this field of grass and all the corn and barley are fit for one thing — burning!'

Billington gasped. 'But you *can't* mean that! It's the mightiest crop in history — and the way the drought is going we're going to need every scrap of staple food we can get!'

'You asked me for an opinion. I'm giving it. Use any of this giant stuff and pass it on for human or animal consumption and you'll commit mass slaughter!'

The officials looked at one another and Drew moved with sudden activity. He kept on moving until he reached the corn again. From it he took several ears, more soil specimens, and finally some samples of barley. By the time they had done this they had returned to the start of the vista where stood the car.

'Where are the giant trees you mentioned?' Drew asked.

'Over here.' Billington motioned and led the way.

In a moment or two the party had reached a derelict structure that had once been a farmhouse. Now only three of its walls were standing. The fourth had obviously been smashed down quite recently by the outjutting branch of a mighty oak. Formerly the tree had been in the shadow behind the glare of floodlights, but now the men stood in the gloom and looked at this colossal giant rearing to heaven with something of the fantastic proportions of Jack's beanstalk.

'I've seen redwoods and sequoia in my time,' Billington said, 'but never anything like this. What makes it queer is that six months ago it was only a small tree ten feet high. Oak is slow-growing as a rule, too . . .'

He craned back his head and followed

the dark, massive trunk as it soared upwards out of sight.

Drew moved position and went over to the tree, inspecting the tip of the lower branches. The others joined him and then slowly became aware of the incredible fact that the tree was growing as they watched it! The branches were swelling and fattening and, though it was well past the spring of the year new leaves were gradually uncoiling and flowing into full life.

'If this gets any higher it will crash through being top-heavy,' Billington remarked. 'There must be something queer about the soil around here.'

'And not only around here,' Drew remarked. 'You mentioned other Areas had been affected in this fashion, didn't you?'

'That's right. But offhand I can't remember which.'

'You'd better find them and tell those in charge to destroy the crops they contain. As for this soil, it's rank poison.'

'Look,' Ken said, his voice anxious. 'What happens if other areas get affected like this? Such as the gigantic fields of Canada, America, Russia, and others? What becomes of our staple food supply?'

'It disappears!' Drew was coldly matter-of-fact. 'We'll have to fall back on synthesis or something. I have got to find out what has gone wrong and try and think of a way to circumvent it in future. Just the same, gentlemen, without wishing to be too depressing, I don't think there *is* a cure. To be honest, I think this trouble will increase ten-fold, hundred-fold, thousand-fold . . . '

'But why?' Billington demanded blankly. 'What's gone wrong?'

'The trouble is K-40, a radioactive isotope of potassium. It was prevalent in the Carboniferous Period — hence the rank growths of that time; and it looks as though it is prevalent again. No more than I expected. It's the direct outcome of cosmic ray activity.'

Drew was silent for a moment, knowing it was useless to explain scientific issues to hidebound officials.

'I'll return home and analyse what I have here,' he said, turning away. 'In the meanwhile, destroy everything as I told you. When I have the full analysis I'll report. After that it will be up to the Government — to every Government in the world, in fact.'

In his walk back to the car he paused and reflected.

'Come to think of it,' he said, 'these samples may not be enough in themselves. I'd better get some more from other affected areas. If they match up in every case then I know the answer is the right one — and I hope to God it isn't!'

'You'd better fly back with me to my office in London,' Billington said. 'I'll have a man get your helicar back to you. In an hour or less I can get you all the details of the affected Areas and then you can make your own arrangements.'

Drew gave his brief nod and resumed his walk to the car. Ken fell into step beside him.

'I'll leave you in London, Anton,' he said. 'I've a lot of work to do tomorrow so I can't go around with you as much as I'd like to. Okay?'

'Of course — and don't forget what I told you about Thayleen. I'm afraid there's the devil of a lot of trouble brewing.'

4

By the evening of the next day Ken had decided that the best way to get Thayleen to cancel her concert tour was for him to go to Paris and talk to her. Over the 'phone he would not sound very convincing. But he was prepared first to watch her concert from Paris over TV; then when it was over he would fly across the Channel.

To his annoyance, however, as he fiddled with the TV set, he only received on a screen a tracery of wavy black bars for vision, whilst through the speaker came ear-cracking static. Paris was completely submerged in electrical disturbance.

He tried for at least five minutes beyond the start of the concert to get results, without success; then as he sat pondering what to do — the speaker's din tuned down to a minimum — his ears caught the distant rumbling of thunder.

Rising he went to the french windows and looked out on the calmness of the evening. Not a leaf moved. The sky was saffron yellow with heat; the visibly spotted sun hung as a deeper golden circle in the mists. Over to the east and north the sky was clear. To the west it was purplish — and to the south violet-black, as though mountain ranges had piled up somewhere within the region of the Channel or the French coast.

'Devil of a storm over in the Paris direction,' Ken muttered to himself. 'That's it! Electrical interference. I might manage the 'phone, though.'

He went to the instrument — just at the very moment when Thayleen was doing likewise, but for her to reach a visiphone was an infinitely harder job than Ken's.

She had had to fight her way through a half-shattered concert hall, her escape from death being occasioned by the fact that she had been alone on the platform and, as the building had been struck by an inconceivably powerful bolt of lightning she had instinctively plunged under

51

the grand piano. It had saved her from the beams and masonry as the roof had caved in.

Behind her now, amidst the cannonade of thunder and smashing of torrential rain she could hear the screams and shouts of the trapped audience, the clanging of alarm bells, the hoarse orders of rescue parties — then she found herself floundering into the partly wrecked manager's office and looked about her for the visiphone. It was undamaged in itself though she had her doubts if the line would be operating.

It not being a public instrument no payment was required. She waited tensely, wincing as lightning suffused the office around her in momentary blue fire; then the voice she heard in the receiver was drowned out by a shattering, ripping thunderclap.

'Help!' she shouted hoarsely. 'Hello! Can you hear me?'

She looked at the blank teleplate. Then the voice came back.

'Who's that? Kenyon West speaking — '

'Ken!' Thayleen cried. 'Thank heaven!

This concert hall is coming down round my ears. There's a terrific storm raging in Paris here. I never saw anything like it.'

'I can hear it,' Ken said, 'and I can see it looks pretty black to the south. You want me to fetch you home?'

'As fast as you can. I'm scared to death — too scared to stay on at my hotel, anyway. You can be here in twenty minutes — but do be careful! Flying in this may be dangerous.'

'No doubt of it, but I'll risk it. Where shall I find you?'

'I'll be at what's left of the stage entrance to the Bijou Concert Hall. Hurry, Ken, please!'

'Rely on it, dearest.'

The line went dead. Thayleen cast a frightened look about her and then found her way out of the office again. The roar of the storm remained undiminished though the lightning did not seem to be concentrating so much on this one spot as hitherto. In the passageway firemen were hurrying towards the shattered hall, carrying hose and ladders

Moving with difficulty in her long

evening gown Thayleen headed for the open doorway of the stage entrance. As she reached it she recoiled, dazzled by a blinding flash of lavender light that seemed to explode in front of her. Her hands to her ears to shut out the deadening concussion of thunder, she reeled back against the wall. Outside, the already torrential rain increased to a flood, turning the back alley into a brimming brook.

'Don't go out, Thayleen. You might be killed.'

At the warning, Thayleen turned in surprise. She looked at a dirty, hatless man in a ripped mackintosh. For a moment, so smothered in drying blood and dirt was his face, she did not recognise him. Then his action of putting a briar between his teeth brought a gasp from her.

'Anton!' she exclaimed. 'How in the world did you get here?'

He grasped her hand warmly. She was trembling violently and her dark eyes looked wild. She looked away sharply and winced as another scaring flash crackled outside and thunder ripping down with it set the building quivering.

'Noisy, isn't it?' Drew murmured, as Thayleen clung to him instinctively for protection. 'I won't be damned fool enough to say there's nothing to be afraid of, because there is. However, this storm should stop as suddenly as it began. Depends on electronic drifts . . . '

A momentary calm interval gave Thayleen courage again. She looked at Drew's dour, blood-streaked face.

'You haven't explained how you found me, Anton — '

'I've been around Europe most of today making agricultural tests. Tonight I decided to drop in here and listen to you. I did — and got mixed up when the roof collapsed. I saw you hurrying to the back regions and chased after you . . . This isn't just a thunderstorm,' Drew continued quietly. 'It's an outburst of cosmic energy, and for that reason it should stop as suddenly as it started.'

'Cosmic energy?' Thayleen looked surprised. 'What has that to do with it?'

'Everything, but it's too involved to explain now.'

A flash of lightning followed by an explosion of thunder — far less violent than before — made Thayleen start.

'What chance do you think a 'plane or a helicar stands in this?' she asked.

'None. Tomorrow we'll hear of thousands of people having been killed in this storm and of aircraft being blasted right out of the sky. You're not thinking of taking a 'plane until this has cleared up, are you?'

'Ken's flying here to get me. I never thought . . . '

Drew looked at the girl for a moment and then turned and hurried to the stage doorway. He peered out into the rain, then up into the sky, most of it dark as midnight even though it was only early evening. But here and there against the angry nimbus were paler gashes where the clouds were breaking.

'I think he'll be all right,' Drew said, returning to where Thayleen was standing. 'The storm's passing. In any case Ken isn't a fool; he'll look after himself. Where did you say you would meet him?'

'Here — at this stage door.'

'Good. He can land in the park out front.'

Thayleen became silent again. She looked towards the far end of the corridor where firemen and gendarmes were at work. Drew struck a match and lighted his pipe; then the girl turned and looked into his pale eyes.

'You're a scientist, Anton,' she said. 'There have been other storms like this, but not as violent. I suppose there is an explanation, apart from hot weather?'

'Of course. It's involved, though.'

'Involved, or do you imagine I wouldn't understand?'

Lightning made the corridor pale amethyst for a moment. Thunder rumbled remotely. Drew went on smoking.

'That's it,' he said. 'I don't think you'd understand. But I do think you should cancel your concert tour and stay home.'

'But I've a contract to fulfil!'

'You sent for Ken to take you home, didn't you?'

'Yes — but I was scared.' Thayleen sighed. 'I realise now I shouldn't have done it. It was only a storm, after all. I'll tell Ken when he comes that I've changed my mind and I'll go to the hotel in the normal way. I'm due to play tomorrow night in the Boulevard Hall — if it's still standing, If I were to break my contract because of thunder I'd be thought a scared little schoolgirl, wouldn't I?'

'Better that than lose your life.'

'What *do* you mean, Anton?'

Drew shrugged. 'I'm talking about the danger of these storms. As I told you, cosmic disturbances are causing them. They will get worse, much worse, until finally few parts of the world will escape them. If a really savage storm breaks you should be at home.'

Thayleen's eyes were steady. 'You're hiding something.'

Drew hesitated; then at the sound of quick footsteps in the rain-gutted alley he turned. Ankle-deep in water, Ken came in, his leather flying jacket black with rain, little rivulets coursing down his face from his saturated hair.

'Ken!' Thayleen hurried forward, embracing him. He kissed her and then looked at Drew in surprise.

'You too, Anton!'

'I just happened to be here. How did you fare?'

'I kept on the storm fringe. I never saw a storm-centre so dense, either. It put all my electric instruments out of action. Paris looks to be in a mess,' Ken finished grimly. 'I counted twelve blazing buildings. All the tall ones seem to have been damaged, and half the Eiffel Tower's gone.'

Drew said nothing. He wandered to the door and looked outside. The rain had ceased. Dirty, scummy clouds were drifting in a rising wind. The air was unpleasant — dank and sulphuric.

'We can risk it now,' he said.

Ken and Thayleen joined him, Thayleen giving a little shiver in the coldness that had come with the storm cessation. She hesitated over saying something to Drew, then thinking better of it she went ahead of Ken down the alley way. They circumvented the front of the smashed edifice, and so crossed the street to Ken's helicar in the park opposite.

They were airborne before anybody

spoke; then Ken turned from the controls.

'Find out all you wanted in Europe, Anton?'

'Yes.'

'I thought you worked for Bland,' Thayleen remarked, puzzled. 'Why are you making agricultural tests in Europe?'

'Routine,' Drew answered.

'I think both of you are holding out on me,' Thayleen said flatly. 'From the miserable look on both your faces one would think the — the end of the world was coming, or something.'

Ken and Drew exchanged looks.

'I'm working for the Government now,' Drew explained. 'I'm sworn to secrecy . . .' Drew switched the subject. 'Congratulations on the baby, Thayleen. I've been too occupied to mention it.'

'Thanks, Anton.' Thayleen was thoughtful. 'I suppose your knowing a baby is coming wouldn't account for you saying I should stay at home?'

'Yes, that's it.' Drew agreed, seizing the opportunity. 'If you get involved in scares like tonight it won't do the youngster much good. Why wreck the chances of the unborn just to fulfil a contract?'

Thayleen was silent. The lights of southern England were approaching. Here there were no storm clouds and the air was fairly clear. Ken turned, murmuring into Drew's ear.

'I think you've convinced her she should stay at home, Anton. What chances are there of the world's end being a mistake?'

'There's no mistake,' Drew muttered. 'The first signs are here with us. The rest is only a question of time.'

*   *   *

The storm which had devastated half Paris moved eastward during the night, then turned back on its tracks and hit London in the early hours. There was hardly a soul in the city who was not kept awake by the terrific thunder and blinding lightning. Each reacted according to temperament

For Thayleen it was a return to terror; to Ken a nightmare in which he tried to maintain a bold front for Thayleen's sake.

To Anton Drew, working through the night in his laboratory, it was the outcome of natural forces, and because he knew just what was transpiring his habitual calm was unshaken.

Particularly scared was Milly Morton. She spent the time from three in the morning until dawn — when the storm began to abate — either hiding her face in a pillow or sitting close to twin reading lamps so their brilliance mitigated the lightning. She was scared enough to make a proposition to Mortimer Bland when she arrived at the Bland Edifice for her usual 'duties'.

Bland himself was looking pasty from a sleepless night, but he was not scared. He had too much bulldog courage for that.

'Morty, I want you to take me away for a vacation until the summer storms have gone.' Milly came right to the point.

Bland sighed. 'Impossible with all the business I have.'

'I insist on it!' Milly added. 'Any more storms like that one last night and I'll go crazy! Haven't you seen the mess it's made of London? It's like those pictures of the 1940 blitz. Smoking rubble, skeleton buildings, hundreds dead — I never before heard of a city being struck by lightning in about a hundred different places. TV news was full of it this morning.'

'I know. Paris had a dose, too — but that's no reason for us to fly off at a tangent.'

'I'm not staying,' Milly declared flatly. 'Besides, in spite of everything, I can't help remembering what Drew said about saving the world. Doesn't it sort of make these storms add up to something?'

Bland started. 'I never thought of it that way.'

'The storm we got last night wasn't the usual bang-and-flash that follows a hot day,' Milly insisted. 'It was hell let loose. I can readily credit a few more like that might mean the end of the world. I want to go somewhere peaceful, where no storms are reported. South America is okay, parts of Canada, southwest United States. Why can't we go on a stratosphere cruise? If the storms cease we'll come back.'

Bland cast an eye towards the window. The morning was sultry and calm after the chaos of the night.

'I'm in two minds whether or not to bring Drew back and make him explain himself,' he said.

'I can see him doing it!' Milly tossed her blonde head in contempt, 'Let's get out and have some comfort.'

Bland's final reluctance went. He grinned and patted Milly's hand as it lay on the desk.

'All right, we'll go. I could do with a vacation, anyway, and especially with you — '

Bland turned abruptly as the visiphone shrilled. As he raised the instrument the face of a man with white moustache appeared on the scanning screen. Bland frowned to himself. It was not often Sir Wilfred Charters, head of the Scientific Association, communicated with him.

'Well, Sir Wilfred, this is unexpected,' Bland said, all pleasantry. 'What can I do for you?'

'Tell me a thing or two about Mr. Drew. He was your head scientist until recently, was he not?'

'Yes indeed.'

'Why did he leave?' the baronet asked. 'I mean did you dismiss him or did he leave of his own accord?'

'He took exception to my secretary,' Bland answered. 'I believe there was some trouble over some photographic plates she accidentally smashed. Drew flew into a rage and left.'

'I see. I just wondered. He has just been here with a most extraordinary story about the end of the world, and he mentioned about some plates he should have had for evidence. He has had a lot to say about K-40, a radioactive isotope of potassium, which is deadly poison and causing a lot of rampant growth up and down the place; and he also had a deal of information concerning cosmic rays. Tell me, Bland, do you think he is — er — Well, *is* he?'

'Crazy?' Bland gave his fleshy chuckle. 'I don't know about that but he's certainly been working hard. So he's worked that end-of-the-world scare on you too, has he? I think it's all damned nonsense.'

'Of course,' the baronet laughed. 'He wants me to summon an army of scientists to discuss matters with him — and a nice fool I'd look if he has to be taken away because of — er — overwork. I'm much obliged, Bland.'

'Don't mention it.' Bland put the instrument down and regarded Milly.

'I hope you know what you're doing,' she said.

'Course I do, m'dear. When it comes to the end of the world 'Wolf!' has been cried far too often . . . '

5

For Thayleen it was a decided effort to follow out Drew's advice and stay at home. With a momentary cessation of storms and return to summer weather she thought less of Drew's advice and more of the contract she had broken, and the law suit which it had invoked. Ken was willing to pay, whatever happened. He considered it worthwhile to keep Thayleen beside him.

Just the same, he and the girl were at loggerheads. They snapped at each other for no apparent reason, quite unaware that they were both suffering from the same dampening of the nervous system that was rife amongst the rank and file of people the world over.

The relentless power of cosmic radiation, slowly becoming stronger as the Earth's magnetic field weakened, was working its own strange changes in the brains and bodies of human beings.

Everybody was incredibly rude following the great Paris and London storms. A crime wave had broken out, too, which the police were not powerful enough to subdue. Even nations who had been friendly were now hurling threats at one another. Slow poison was seeping down on the world, side by side with blazing sunlight in the western hemisphere, and savage frosts in the eastern. In various parts of the world huge growths were springing up — fantastic, beyond all reason.

Then a farmer found the Goliath beetle, and for a couple of days it became of interest to a people harassed and perplexed by forces they could not understand.

A beetle three feet long and two feet high had come to a Devon village. Nobody knew its origin, but apparently two farmhands had slain it. They were heroes. The image of the dead beetle was televised throughout the globe.

Had the business stayed at one beetle it would have just been one of those things, but the day afterwards several more were found in widely separated districts. In Europe there were not only giant beetles but wasps and bees as well, the wasps having a sting virulent enough to kill a strong man in an hour. The insects flew so rapidly and so intelligently it was hard to shoot them down.

These occurrences, which seemed to be connected with reports of giant ants, worms as big as snakes and stagnant ponds choked with ever-expanding life — which had crawled out amidst waist-high nettles and grass — began to have a meaning for even the dullest intellect.

Anton Drew heard of these happenings and made a note of them. He also heard of others, much more horrible, of which the public knew nothing. Yet apparently no scientist acted. Drew could not understand it, waiting as he was for Sir Wilfred Charters to convene a meeting.

To Thayleen, when she heard — and saw televised pictures — of the giant insects and worms, there was a feeling of nightmare instead of actual horror. As though the world were turning inside out and she could do nothing to stop it.

In a vast endeavour to escape from the monotony of home she began to take long walks through the surrounding country-side. On the fourth day, to try and prevent an estrangement, Ken went with her, deliberately absenting himself from his work to do so.

They spoke little as they tramped through the coarse, knee-high grass. It seemed preposterous, but here and there they caught sight of flowers they had never seen before — huge purple things with poisonous green stems, their enor-mous heads shooting over the grass and emitting a foul odour.

When Ken and Thayleen had reached a point of the field where there was a dip that gave a clear view of London, they settled down — to find the view of London had gone. They had dropped into a hollow where the grass swept up and waved seven feet above their heads.

'Ken — ' Thayleen looked around on the shady grass forest. 'Ken — I'm getting frightened! Honestly, I am!'

Ken was glad to find her turning to

him as she had used to do before they had bitten each other's heads off.

'Probably your nerves, dear — your contract and — '

'Nothing of the sort!' Thayleen's voice was hard. 'It's things like *this*! And beetles, ants, wasps, and worms — everything behaving as it shouldn't. Decent people committing loathsome crimes! Everything crawling, beastly, and big! Big — ! *Hideously big!* Even *I'm* different'! I even look it.'

'Imagination,' Ken smiled.

'No, it isn't! I'm not as good-looking as I used to be. That isn't meant to be egotistical, either.' Thayleen mused over this, her eyes on the weird grass against the brazen summer sky. 'You know yourself I've always been a good-looking girl. But now my skin is thickening and I feel beastly!'

Ken did not speak. For the first time, he realised that she was right. She was different, but the change in her had been so subtly wrought he had been at a loss to account for it.

'Look at my hands!' She held them

forward. 'The hands of Thayleen West. As coarse as a char's!'

'Yes,' Ken whispered. 'They *are* different — '

'And *you* are different!' Thayleen said. 'Coarser and more bulbous, and if it didn't sound too utterly preposterous I'd say your hair is growing lower down on to your forehead — Ken, what is wrong with everybody? I'm sure you can explain it. Anton's told you something, hasn't he?'

'Yes,' Ken admitted, setting his big mouth. 'And I don't see why I should keep it back anymore. He believes in all seriousness that the end of the world is coming — Not one vast explosion in which we'd all blow up and finish it — but something slow, relentless, devastating. I've gathered enough to know that sunspots started it — '

'End — of — the — world?' Thayleen repeated the words slowly.

As near as he could, Ken related the theory of the magnetic field, and concluded:

'The storms, the mad vegetation, the giant insects the change in human beings

— they're all caused by increasing cosmic radiation.'

'Why did he insist on my staying at home?'

'So you could protect yourself. He suspects worse storms than we've had so far.'

'There was no other reason?'

'None that I know of, Thay. If you were involved in a disastrous storm whilst away, and I was in London, we'd never meet again this side of Eternity.'

'End of the world,' Thayleen said again. 'It's so unbelievable. We take the world for granted and plan accordingly. How long does Anton give before the end comes?'

'He hasn't said.'

'But the future! Our baby! Thousands of babies — '

Ken did not speak. The hot wind stirred the screen of grass; then at a sudden croaking he and Thayleen looked up in surprise. They had a glimpse of a gigantic toad, its eyes staring fixedly, its throat pulses beating. Then it had gone. For the first time, they had been brought face to face with a product of this new-old Age of the Big that was just commencing.

'One thing I do know,' Ken said. 'We've got to have this out with Anton and get the facts.'

'I gather I wasn't told anything at first because Anton had the impudence to think I couldn't keep a secret?'

It was the second time Ken had been surprised by Thayleen's acid tone. It sounded like another girl speaking.

'I don't think he looked at it that way, Thay. He just didn't want a panic to start, and you had inadvertently — '

'I'll tell Anton what I think of him when I see him! And I can't think of a better time than now.'

Thayleen swung away and went climbing up the grass bank. Ken followed her, and without speaking they returned home through the waist-high wilderness. Worried and hot, Ken got out his car; and, beyond saying he was ready to go, he added no further comment to the taut-featured, nervy girl who flung herself in the seat beside him.

Fifteen minutes ride through the dusty

countryside incredibly changed with its rank vegetation and dried-up ponds, then another ten minutes of slow crawling through congested streets, brought them to the building where Drew had his flat. He opened the door himself, and they both stood motionless for a moment, shocked at the change in him.

His hair had gone greyer: his features were thicker.

'Hello,' he greeted, in his usual casual fashion. 'Come in. It's damned untidy, but I've no time for trifles.' He held the door wide, then took his pipe from his teeth and followed Ken and the girl into the living room.

'What brings you here this time of day?' he asked

'Everything!' Thayleen retorted. 'Why couldn't you trust me with your end-of-the-world secret? We've been friends since we stole apples together, haven't we?'

Drew's pale eyes strayed to Ken and he gestured a little.

'I had to tell her, Anton. She can see for herself. And look at us. How different we are.'

'Yes,' Drew muttered. 'Devolution — atavism — has set in.'

'Meaning — what?' Thayleen looked at him in surprise.

'I mean, my dear, that you, Ken, and I — and every living being in the world — are no longer evolving normally. We are sliding backwards. Those who are being born are abnormal to start with, hence the giant insects, and so forth which is the direct result of cosmic radiation on the germ plasm of the parent. It's a ghastly business,' Drew finished wearily.

'Why didn't you *trust* me?' Thayleen demanded angrily.

Drew shrugged. 'I didn't even trust Ken, let alone you. I even slipped myself, in admitting the world was finished. If I could do it, so could Ken, so could you. One word out of season might have blown order higher than a kite. Forget it, Thayleen. Everybody must see by now that something is coming.'

'Haven't you contacted anybody about it yet?' Ken asked.

'Four days ago, I asked the head of the

Scientific Association to get the world's scientists together so I could explain matters. Nothing's happened — which shows what it means to have an ignoramus pushed into position through influence. I don't think the damned fool understood a word I said!'

'It does take a lot of swallowing,' Ken reflected.

'He can't laugh off what's happening now,' Drew replied sourly. 'What's probably clouding his judgment is my inability to produce my solar plates, thanks to that fool secretary of Bland's, who smashed them. If I don't get satisfaction by five tonight, I'm going to see the Prime Minister. There has got to be quick action.'

'Why don't other scientists say something?' Thayleen asked in bewilderment. 'They must know what is going on.'

'Of course; but without the sanction of Sir Wilfred Charters, they couldn't possibly speak publicly. If they do so, they are finished, as a doctor who acts unethically. For myself, I don't care what happens to me as long as the truth is made known. The Prime Minister may grasp the importance of things.'

'All this apart,' Thayleen said, after a pause, 'how does cosmic radiation make us slide backwards?'

'Because change is going on within us all the time. We are adding cells and losing them. Our energy is constantly fluctuating — anabolism and ketabolism, it is called — and our bloodstreams undergo constant variations, thinning in heat and thickening in cold. Those are normal changes inherent on a living being, and they are changes that affect the brain, since it is fed by the bloodstream. With the increase in cosmic-ray activity, all the normal functions are upset, and the unpredictable happens. It causes a thickening of the cells forming the skin; it reacts on the gland structure, and, in the males, brings a change of hair formation. To sum it up, we are not progressing because evolution has been halted by excessive cosmic energy. We are, in a sense, de-volving insofar that the development we normally have is thrown right out of gear and we are assuming characteristics of the lower orders.'

'At times, I have the uncontrollable urge to run,' Thayleen said. 'That part of the trouble?'

'Uh-huh,' Drew sighed. 'The effect on adult beings is bad enough, but on the young and unborn it will be worse. In the young, these violent changes will produce unheard of consequences because the young are mutating from one stage to another. With glandular and other systems exposed to cosmic radiation, we can expect not human beings in the next generation but travesties of them! Freaks! In the unborn, the same trouble will arise, and the result will be — I don't know what. The normal child will be the exception.'

'Which means,' Ken said slowly, 'that our child when born, may be — '

'Possibly.' Drew looked at Thayleen as she remained white and silent, sitting on a nearby chair. 'I know how you must feel. In common with everybody, you are in the midst of the worst blight which ever hit the Earth. If only it ended there we might find a way round the problem, but that isn't the worst of it.'

'What more *can* there be?' Ken's voice was outraged.

'Our very existence,' Drew answered, 'will eventually be threatened by the insect and animal kingdom! With increasing cosmic radiation, that infernal K-40 isotope of potassium with which Earth's surface is being dusted will thicken. Inevitably, animals will absorb it. Its effect will be to produce giantism and ferocity, where it does not produce death. It was the prevalence of K-40, which gave us the giant beasts and forests of the prehistoric ages: it will inevitably come again. New-born elephants, for instance, the germ plasm of the parents being affected, will be mastodons and mammoths.

'The tiger will become the sabre-tooth; certain species of lizards will become pterodactyls. So it will go on. The giant insects already seen and destroyed are samples of that which is to come. Trees, grass, soaking in potassium isotope, will expand to undreamed-of size, smashing down everything man has ever built up.

Choked oceans, swarming with ever-increasing life. The list is endless.'

'And we take it all?' Ken asked grimly. 'Man has the highest intelligence, and he's been called upon now to use it as never before. There must be a way out! How about space travel to get to another world? Thousands of space machines could be built rapidly if the governments of the developed countries pooled and concentrated their resources.'

'True, and I daresay they could if we really set about it — but it wouldn't be any use. There are no planets that can support human life, and even if there were, their magnetic fields must be in the same state as the Earth. They all obey the master-gravity of the sun, and thereby will be affected by this sunspot rash. Possibly the effect may be slower on the rim of the Solar System. But to transport a chosen number of humans to the outer deeps — where they couldn't possibly survive outside of a protected environment — would be ridiculous.' Drew shook his untidy head. 'Our fight is *here*! And there is only one answer. Go underground.'

'How deep?' Thayleen asked.

'That would have to be worked out. I have suggestions for underground cities if I can get a hearing. The trouble is that the heavier cosmic rays penetrate thirty feet of lead and over a hundred feet of solid rock, so we'd at least have to go below that depth to find security. If we could succeed in creating underground cities, it would mean that you and I, and other adults, would end our lives down there. Only the unborn — as yet — would eventually emerge to the surface with the passing of the sunspot phase.' Drew paused for a moment, and then added: '*If it passes* — '

'You said a century,' Ken reminded him.

'I know; but the possibility of a solar collapse into a white dwarf is not improbable with so many increasing spots. That would make the surface uninhabitable for all time. The world would be sheathed in a cocoon of ice. However that is peering too far into a dismal future. The job at the moment is to get action from the world's various governments. I'll try and contact Sir Wilfred later in the day.'

★ ★ ★

To Milly Morton, on the fourth day of the stratosphere cruise — aboard Mortimer Bland's private jet plane — life was just heavenly, in more senses than one. From London they had hopped at stratosphere level to Pernambuco in Brazil, had stayed a night in languorous warmth and calm climate; and from there had hurtled to San Francisco. On the way they had glimpsed incredible fields of grass and grain, and seen traces of where storms had struck with savage violence — but they themselves experienced nothing unusual, and 'Frisco could not have been more tranquil.

Now they were heading south-eastwards again on the longest hop of all — non-stop to New Delhi and the Orient.

Bland's strato-jet plane was run on much the same lines as a millionaire's yacht — a crew taking charge of the technical side, and he and Milly occupying the luxurious quarters in the centre of the machine. Here, apart from living and sleeping quarters, there was everything they needed from a swimming pool, solarium, and gymnasium, to tennis and badminton courts, gyroscopic control maintaining everything on a dead level.

Definitely Milly was having the time of her life. So was Bland, for that matter, his only worry being that whilst away he had left a laboratory assistant in charge of his affairs. The man was trustworthy enough, but he was no Anton Drew. However, acceding to Milly's demands was Bland's chief concern, so he thought as little as possible about upheavals in his organisation in far-away England.

Here, in the stratosphere, so close to its rim that the sky was no longer blue but violet, there were occasions when both Bland and Milly found themselves looking at the sun — not with the naked eye but through the dense purple goggles they wore when in the solarium. Usually, from here, one could see the sun's magnificent corona and prominences — but these no longer impressed, fantastic though they were. It was the *face* of the sun that held attention.

It looked like a globe at which somebody had flung handfuls of mud. Right down to the solar poles the areas of devouring darkness stretched, obscuring more than a third of the blinding photosphere. It was a sight at once ugly and horrifying, one on which Milly certainly did not care to dwell. It reminded her too much of Drew's ambiguous warning.

What the crew thought of the solar disk was not known, but it was plain that they had no particular liking for this stratosphere flight, for the simple reason that their instruments were all awry. Though they had no knowledge of cosmic-ray activity — since the news had not yet leaked out to the world in general — they were remembering the frightful magnetic storms that had burst upon Earth at intervals, and the thought of running into one of them was oppressive.

Nothing unusual seemed to happen, however, and the radio reports — blurred with static though they were — gave indications of more or less fair flying weather all the way across the Indian Ocean to New Delhi.

But long before New Delhi was reached, other things happened — to Milly and Bland — and these things began after both of them had spent a lazy afternoon in the solarium together, divested of all clothing to the limits of decency.

During the night, as the plane swept onwards, Milly was awakened by the feeling that somebody was throwing boiling water upon her. Seared with pain from head to foot, she flung out a quivering hand and snapped on the beside light. Then she threw off the coverlet.

Appalled, her nerves torn with anguish, she stared at a series of monstrous blisters covering every portion of her skin. They had risen on her legs, her arms, her shoulders — everywhere she looked and touched. To even move was agony; but with Milly her appearance came first, so she forced herself out of bed and stumbled as though on red-hot coals to the full-length mirror.

Her reflection nearly stunned her — Her face was a mass of flaming scars and hideous burns. Her eyes had nearly vanished in thickened flesh. Her mouth and cheeks looked as though they had flowed into each other. She raised one leg of her satin pyjamas and revealed a shapeless mass of flesh rather like raw beef. The sight was so astounding she gave one shriek, and then, overcome with pain and fear she dropped in a dead faint to the floor.

She might have lain there for hours, only Bland himself similarly affected, was on the move. Since his personal beauty was his last thought, he did not collapse on seeing himself in the mirror. Instead, wincing with pain, he pressed the bell for attention, and presently his personal valet, hastily dressed, came into the room.

'Get Dr. Williams,' Bland panted, drenched in perspiration. 'I'm ill, or something. Burning like hell.'

The valet stared at the amazing sight his master presented.

'And — and find out if Miss Morton's

all right,' Bland added, breathing hard. 'If she isn't, tell Williams.'

'Right away, Mr. Bland.' And the valet hurried out.

That began it. Dr. Williams, paid a preposterous sum to compensate for removing him from his practice whilst he stood by for possible mishaps aboard Bland's flyer, found himself with two complicated cases on his hands. His first order was to have the plane grounded in Bombay, and here the groaning, stricken tycoon and the girl were taken to hospital.

It was three days before the pain began to abate, and then each of them realised they were smothered in medicated wadding and were being fed at intervals as though they were babies.

Bland's first demand was to know what in blue hell had happened and Williams — who had no liking for the great man and his loose habits — did not mince his answers.

'Cosmic radiation burns,' he explained, looming over the tycoon's bedside. 'You and Miss Morton must have soaked yourselves in them or something. There isn't a square inch on either of your bodies that escaped it. You're lucky you are not both stone blind, too.'

'We had good sun-glasses,' Bland wheezed.

'They saved your eyes, then. As for the burns, you'll be all right in a day or so. I got them treated just in time.' Williams paused, and then added: 'The cruise has got to stop, Mr. Bland. That's my advice.'

'Stop? Stop, be damned! We've only just started! We're going on for several weeks yet, until the end of the summer. If we keep off the sun-bathing we'll be all right, won't we?'

'Sun-bathing has nothing to do with your trouble. You and the girl didn't get excessive sunburn; it was cosmic radiation that blasted you. Not being a scientist, I can't explain why, through glass specially polarised to counteract cosmic rays at extreme heights, you should have been so affected; but I must warn you that the crew has also been affected by burns, to a lesser degree. I have myself. Stratosphere cruising is no longer safe. The crew is grumbling.'

89

'Okay,' Bland growled, relaxing. 'Can't go on without a crew, I suppose. And I was just starting to enjoy myself! What about the girl? How's she going on?'

'About the same as you, but though I've got the burns down, she looks very different to what she did.'

Bland muttered something inaudible, and then said no more. Thereafter, he was confined to bed for several more days; and things were not improved by a storm which burst over New Delhi on the second night, and turned the great Eastern city into a bewildering chaos of exploding lightning, shattering thunder, vastly heavy rainfall, and tottering buildings.

Then at last Bland was able to rise again, and for the time being took a suite in the Pinnacle Hotel. Here he saw Milly for the first time since the solarium sunbathing. He could not believe what he saw. From his own appearance in the mirror, he knew he himself was different, with thickened skin and unusually heavy increase in hair growth — but with Milly it was as though she were another woman entirely.

Her graceful lines had gone. She was as heavy as a dowager and had put on several stones in weight. A new outfit of clothes — obviously for a woman several sizes larger than she had been — was by no means a happy choice with its Eastern-flower flamboyance. It made her look worse. Her exposed arms, scarred where the burns had been, were unpleasant to look at, but her face was the biggest shock. It was flat and blunt-featured, the mouth somewhat askew only the teeth and eyes remaining as of yore — when they could be seen. The blonde hair had become lank and silver-grey.

Bland absorbed the sight and then sat down heavily.

'Great heavens,' he whispered.

Milly settled in a chair and looked at him fixedly.

'All right, laugh,' she invited him stonily. 'Something happened to us when we sun-bathed. I'm ugly as a gargoyle, five stones heavier, and I feel terrible. But for your confounded stratosphere cruise this would never have happened to me!'

'But you suggested it!' Bland cried, astonished.

'The cruise, yes — but not the sun-bathing. That was your idea. And look what happened!'

'You don't have to blame it on me. It just happened, and when I get back to London I'll sue the makers of that radiation-proof glass in the solarium. It's no damned good!'

Bland considered Milly for a moment, and then he added: 'As for us, Milly, we're washed up. Finished!'

'Are we?' Milly's voice was ominous. 'More bluntly you mean that because I've lost the looks and figure you raved about, you're kicking me out. That's it, isn't it?'

'Yes. I'll get you back to London, and that's all.'

'You try kicking me out, Mort, and I'll — '

'No, you won't,' Bland shook his head deliberately. 'You don't suppose anybody would think that a hag like you is the original Milly Morton, showgirl, do you? No Milly. Whilst you were the Milly Morton of the looks and figure, you had a

92

weapon in your hand, because you could prove you were the girl I had been associating with. That doesn't hold good any more. You can say and do what you like, but with everything about you so changed you'll get nowhere.'

'That doctor can prove I'm Milly Morton so can the crew of your flyer. I'll bring an action for damages and — '

'Try it,' Bland suggested, shrugging. 'I happen to know that the witnesses you need can be bought off — and they will be. I've been waiting for a long time to get rid of you, Milly, and this is it. You're a two-timing little blackmailer. Fight me, if you like, but I'll beat you. I have the money and the influence.'

Milly said nothing for a while. She sat and glared. Then at last, with a setting of her ugly mouth, she got to her feet. She left the room and slammed the door.

6

In the days whilst Bland and Milly had languished in hospital in New Delhi, Anton Drew had been fighting his battles, too. Commencing with a passage-at-arms with Sir Wilfred Charters — which did little to improve Drew's chances — Drew had gone to the Prime Minister, to find that he was out of town.

With increasing desperation, he spent three days trying to contact other scientists and officials. In some cases he was successful — as far as the scientists were concerned — but the government officials were not even remotely interested. In fact, Sir Wilfred's comment that Drew was suffering from overwork did irreparable harm.

So, finally, Drew went back to his laboratory, fuming, taking with him the valuable data he had left with Sir Wilfred in the hopes he would summon a convention.

Had the issue been that of the government alone — or the scientists who were tied down by the regulations of the Scientific Association — Drew would have troubled no more, and instead would have taken precautions solely to preserve himself and his few intimate friends. But he was too conscientious to take this viewpoint, too aware of the manner in which the rank and file of the people were being exposed to deadly danger through the dim-mindedness of the leaders.

A couple of hours brought Drew to a decision. He waited until nightfall; then, with a revolver in his pocket, he took a stroll as far as the Prime Minister's private residence. He avoided the front of the building, where two constables were on duty, and instead crept upon the house from the back. There were constables here, too, at various points, but by moving in absolute silence and in total darkness — for the sky was sombrely overcast and smelled of another storm to come — he managed to circumvent them. His knock on the rear door of the house brought a servant to open it. With the gun in his hand, Drew found the remainder easy. In a few moments he was shown by the alarmed manservant into the Prime Minister's study.

Far from being out of town, he was working at his desk, the single fan of light casting on the blotter and deflecting to his austere features.

'Good evening, Mr. Drew,' he greeted, his eyes straying from the gun to Drew's grim face. 'You may go Benson', he added to the manservant.

'I think not,' Drew snapped. 'I'm not giving him the chance to call the police. Sit over there, Benson. As one of the rank and file, you may as well hear what I have to say — then you'll know who is to blame if you get killed in the disaster which is coming.'

The Prime Minister sat back in his chair and watched the servant settle uneasily on a chair in the corner.

'I'm surprised that a man of your professional standing, Mr. Drew, should descend to the level of a gangster,' the Prime Minister commented.

'And it surprises me, sir, that you should invent the paltry excuse of being out of town rather than listen to me.'

Drew retorted: 'I assume you took that step because of the remarks of Sir Wilfred Charters. I know what he is saying — that I am unbalanced through overwork.'

'Your present behaviour would seem to confirm it.'

Drew settled at the desk and put his briefcase upon it with his free hand. From it he took the evidence and pushed it across the blotter.

'Now,' Drew said, 'you have got to listen to me even if it is at the point of a gun. I know I'm running foul of the law, but there seems no other way. Unless you act fast the people of this country are going to revolt because of Government inaction in face of death. Not only you, but every leader in the world has got to listen. And these are the facts — '

Drew gave them in detail, almost a monotonous recital so many times had he repeated them to different people

' . . . so in time everything will become

radioactive,' he concluded. 'The high-energy electrons created by the cosmic waves are the same lightweight negative particles which, in a laboratory, are trained on various elements to make them emit neutrons. It is these neutrons that are the trouble. Being two thousand times heavier than electrons, they are capable of making stable elements radioactive, and when that happens on a large scale the result is plain to foresee.'

'And you believe,' the Prime Minister asked, thinking, 'that the cosmic rays will break through sufficiently to cause that trouble?'

'I'm convinced of it. Giant crops, insects, and so forth, are the visible signs of it. And we ourselves are different. You must be aware of physical changes which are anything but pleasant ones?'

'Certain changes, yes. I have asked some scientists about them, and they suspect sunspots.'

'They are right. The sunspots are weakening our protection against cosmic radiation.'

'And you think our only way to survive

is to dig deeply into the earth and establish a city — or cities?'

'I do. We, and the Governments of other countries, must concentrate exclusively on the task before it is too late.'

The Prime Minister considered. 'Do you suppose any good might be served by mass evacuation to another planet?'

'That idea is useless. All the planets are unsuitable for human life, and in any case they will be in the same condition as Earth so far as radiation is concerned.'

'Then cosmic rays are not solely confined to this planet of ours?'

Drew gave a sigh at the scientific ignorance of the leader of the Government.

'Cosmic rays, sir,' he replied, 'are prevalent throughout our solar system, and far beyond it. Nobody knows quite what they are or where they originate. They were once conceived of as a by-product of the primeval explosion of a single mass of matter, and that from it stellar bodies were formed, being hurled away from that central point in remote space. Recent tests, though, show that

99

other sources of cosmic rays are closer to home than that.'

'Could one perhaps find their source and destroy it?'

'Nobody knows where the source is,' Drew replied dryly. 'If they originate outside the Milky Way — our own Galaxy — there would be certain variations in their intensity but there are not. That means they must originate as free particles somewhere within our Galaxy. They may even be stepped up to cosmic energy by the magnetic fields of double stars in the same way that man-made cyclotrons speed up particles by repeated electrical pushes. Quite possibly some cosmic rays originate in supernova explosions. No, sir, to find the source is impossible, I'm afraid, so the only alternative is to guard against the danger as well as we possibly can.'

'And beyond these evidences of giant insects, thickening of the human skin, and storms, what other evidence of cosmic ray damage will there be?'

'As the cosmic radiation becomes more intense the storms will become more violent, and vegetation will correspondingly be showered with increasing amounts of potassium isotope, created by cosmic rays themselves. Stable elements will become radioactive. Not only grass, grown out of all normal size, will glow at night, but also rocks, mountains and the oceans. Grass will force its way through the strongest plastic and stone. Areas that are now empty will become impassable jungles. Every city in the world is bound, finally, to be strangled by an advancing tide of vegetation, against which we shall be helpless. We must go below. Order Sir Wilfred to convene the scientists and let me talk to them. Let the engineers join us. Inform other Governments of my findings.'

'You say that the solar plates so necessary to prove the extension of sunspots have been destroyed, Mr. Drew?'

'Accidentally, yes; but it is of no great consequence, with so many proofs around us.'

Drew paused, surprised as a hand touched his shoulder. He looked up with a start, into the face of a constable. 'If you don't mind, sir,' the constable said, motioning Drew to rise.

Drew obeyed slowly, bewildered. He caught sight of the Prime Minister's austere face.

'I engaged you in conversation, Mr. Drew, to make an opportunity for my servant to escape and get help. I am sorry that a man of your accomplishments should so break the law as to enter my home with a gun in his hand but evidently this — this delusion of yours has carried you beyond prudence.'

'Delusion!' Drew shouted, colouring. 'Great heavens, don't you see the evidence all around you? You surely don't think I made up a story like that? The changes in us — '

'Quite so,' the Prime Minister broke in gravely. 'Changes which scientists ascribe to sunspot activity, and which will cease as the sunspots diminish. Your rather terrifying picture of the world's end is theatrical in its magnificence, but it is not convincing. Later, when you have rested, I think you will return and admit that fact.'

'But you can't mean — '

'We'd better be on our way, sir,' the constable intervened. 'The charges are unlawful entry and use of firearms.'

Drew snatched his arm free of the constable's grip and whipped up the data he had put on the desk. He jammed it back into the briefcase, then because he could do nothing else he went with the constable. There was a rumble of thunder as he went to the waiting police car.

That night hell broke loose again over London.

From midnight until dawn, the magnetic storm that had gathered during the evening raged with terrifying fury over the capital, completely dwarfing the earlier onslaught both in duration and violence. Nor was it confined to London. Reports showed that it stretched as far south as Belgium and France, and as far north as Birmingham. Everywhere within this radius was hammered and pounded by lightning bolts, together with weird electrical displays never before seen in a storm.

Cameramen who braved the chaos for

the sake of their newsreel companies, obtained their pictures but died in the process. Nothing could live outside in the overwhelming fury of electricity that discharged itself from convulsed and flickering skies. Rain, hurricane, wind, deafening thunder, and incessant lightning all seemed to be mixed up together in one vast fury that kept a shuddering city awake throughout the night.

Anton Drew, in a prison cell for the night until he should be brought before the magistrates to answer the charge against him, was as much aware of the storm as anybody. Most of the time he lay on his bunk listening to its savagery, not caring very much if the building fell on top of him. He had done his best and finished up behind bars.

Thayleen, with memories of her Paris experience still fresh in her mind, was inconsolable as the storm raged to its roaring climax — and there was nothing that Ken, equally scared, could do to reassure her. Then, by dawn, the storm faded and exhausted clouds drifted away in the smoking-hot wind. Thayleen half-lay on the settee in the lounge, her fingers still working spasmodically with nervous reaction.

In the storm areas workers went to their business the following morning through streets that had become rubble overnight. On either side of them were shattered buildings and, even more extraordinary, queer livid green growths, which had grown with incredible speed amidst the ruins and seemed to be expanding in the sullen heat of a misty sun. A queer sun, too, its light vaguely dimmed, a third of its surface blotted out with scars.

The air stank of burning, smouldering rubber and wood, and death. Even the most unimaginative began to ask what was happening. The fury of the night had driven home the realisation that the world was no longer what it had been any more than were human beings themselves.

The radio-television networks spent the day giving news and views of the night's havoc. It appeared the onslaught had not been confined to southern England and parts of Europe. It had also struck in areas of Sweden, Canada, the United States, South America, and Australia.

And, towards noon the following day, the clouds gathered again — and though not so violent as the hell of the night, another climatic upheaval broke loose. It had hardly cleared long enough to permit shaken workers getting home after an interrupted day's work before, towards eight in the evening, the sky dimmed again to near-midnight blackness and a stillness ghastly beyond imagining settled over the land.

Thayleen and Ken, making a pretence of having a late dinner, kept eating, apprehensive eyes towards the open French windows. The garden which a few weeks before had been their pride, was now a soggy, churned-up mass, half under water. And from the dampness sprouted rampant unclassified growths, which were rapidly strangling everything else in sight. At the moment it was all dim and grey and uncertain. The mellow calm of the past weeks had vanished in this almost perpetual storm centre. Bank upon bank, killing a sunlight that was already wan, the clouds reared up to highest heaven.

'Ken, I can't bear it again,' Thayleen whispered, staring in fascination into the still, unnatural twilight. 'Last night, then this afternoon, and again now — I can't! I *can't*! It's sheer torture! I'll go crazy — '

She broke off, and Ken, too, held his answer, for at that moment a huge bee — nearly as big as an owl — droned into the room from the twilight. It swept round once, batting against the cornice and ceiling, and then went out again. It seemed like a vaguely evil portent of the change destroying the very foundations of life.

'How right Anton was,' Ken said quietly. 'And yet he does nothing. I can't make head or tail of it.'

'Unless,' Thayleen responded, dragging her gaze from the darkening scene outside, 'he's been trying to get the Government to act — and that takes time. Let's see if TV has anything to tell us.'

Ken went across to the set and switched it on. The screen was blank with static bars of shadow. The sound was tinny and unnatural with electrical interference — but through it there did float the voice of the announcer.

' . . . and apparently the storms are increasing in violence and extent in all parts of the world. The Airmet office find it impossible to forecast them, since they do not follow known tracks, and having nothing to do with hot and cold fronts. At the moment it appears that London and seven other cities are threatened with another storm, and similar reports have come in from abroad — '

The sound actually seemed to fizz for a moment as in the distance a brilliant streamer of forked lightning ripped down the black sky and exploded beyond the horizon. Thayleen shut her eyes, her face deathly. Her hands were gripping the table edge in front of her and she held on to it whilst it sounded as though the heavens were being ripped apart. Out of the chaos of subsiding thunder-blast, the announcer's voice drifted back.

' . . . and for this unwarranted entry into the residence of the Prime Minister,

Drew was committed to prison and was today charged by the magistrates with unlawful entry and illegal possession and use of firearms — together with a further charge of using threats to a leader of the State. His case has been referred to a later hearing and — '

The voice stopped, jammed by static as a discharging electrical sluice overhead blew away the chimney stack supporting the aerial, filling the room with amethyst fire. Thayleen screamed and jumped up blindly. She tripped over the rug and crashed upon it, lying flat and shuddering. Ken stumbled over to her as the house rocked with the concussion of the thunder and the electric light extinguished.

He and Thayleen gripped each other, plunged into a vortex of whirling lavender lights, drowned in a cascade of thunderclaps that battered and roared through the flashing darkness with ever-increasing fury.

'Take it easy, Thay,' Ken implored as he felt her struggling. 'What on earth are you trying to do?'

'Let me go Ken,' she insisted, tearing free of his grip — and for a split second amidst the lightning he caught a glimpse of her racing for the French windows, then the blackness clamped down again and thunder belched out of it.

Ken lost precious seconds trying to understand what Thayleen had done — then, as it dawned on him that she was alone and unprotected in the hell outside, he, too, hurtled for the French windows into the garden.

'Thay!' he screamed hoarsely, cupping his hands. 'Thay! For heaven's sake come back — !'

It was impossible for him to make his voice heard over the din. He looked about him, rain swamping down into his face, the flickering, exploding sky above him entirely disregarded. His own safety was his least concern now; it was Thayleen who mattered. He swung round, then fell back as a dazzling flash detonated in front of him. Paralysing cramp nailed his limbs and he crashed half-senseless upon his face, scarcely able to move.

And while he lay, Thayleen was running

through the storm — not blindly, but with a fixed objective. Some miracle seemed to preserve her, for she was never once hit by the lightning, or struck by falling trees as she floundered on her way along the main road. She just kept on going, along lanes which had become quagmires, through fields where the lashing, soaking grass was as high as her shoulders, coming ever nearer to the outskirts of London.

Until, an hour after she had dashed from home, she was hammering fiercely on the door of the Prime Minister's residence. The two constables on duty, despite the fury of the elements, came over and seized her arms. She sagged, half-exhausted in their grip.

'I've *got* to see the Prime Minister!' she insisted. 'I must! I *must!*'

The door opened and the constables tried to decide what to do. Thayleen decided it for them. Tearing out of their grip, she stumbled into the dark hall, all electricity having failed throughout the city, and headed for what she took to be a line of light under a nearby door.

'A moment, madam — ' the servant cried after her, alarmed.

Thayleen was not listening. She flung the door open and hurried into the room beyond. The Prime Minister, at his desk, and using an old-fashioned oil light, looked up sharply as she came in — then to the servant and constables who had followed.

'I have got to see you, sir!' she cried. 'It's about Anton Drew! You must listen to me — '

'That's about enough,' one of the constables snapped. 'You had better — '

'No,' the Prime Minister interrupted. 'Let the lady remain. Benson, pour a glass of brandy for her. Now, madam, please be seated.'

Thankfully, Thayleen sat down, fighting for breath, tossing back saturated hair from her forehead. The constables went out, their capes gleaming, and thunder cracked viciously as the servant poured the brandy. Thayleen took the glass in a shaking hand. She felt better with the spirit coursing through her.'

'I'm afraid the electricity failure makes

me unable to provide any warmth, Mrs. West,' the Prime Minister said, signalling the servant to depart.

'I'm not cold,' Thayleen said. 'You — recognise me then?'

'I could hardly fail to. I have had the pleasure of seeing and hearing you play many times. This is not perhaps a propitious moment to mention your music, but I thank you for it just the same.'

'My music belongs to the past,' Thayleen said dully. 'I am here for one thing only — to discuss Anton Drew. He is a close friend of my husband's, and I just couldn't believe it when I heard over the radio that he had been put in jail. Since you will be the one to press the charges, I beg of you to release him, for the sake of everybody in the world. The world is dying, sir! Can you not see it?'

'So Mr. Drew has told you that story, too?'

'Yes, and because I know him, I believe it.'

'Am I to assume that it is for his sake that you have made such a dangerous trip to see me?'

113

'Partly. I have another reason. As a citizen, I have the right to demand protection from these upheavals when I know there is a man who can give it. Anton Drew, of course.'

'Mr. Drew's evidence of his theory is incomplete — '

'Because a fool of a woman smashed his plates? I know about that.'

'For another thing,' the Prime Minister added, 'Sir Wilfred Charters, of the Scientific Association, is convinced that Mr. Drew is — well, overwrought.'

Thayleen stared. 'You can sit there with this fury going on around us and call Drew overwrought?' she demanded. 'Don't his name and distinguished career count for anything?'

'I am bound by the decision of the majority, madam. Other scientists have not the same views as Mr. Drew.'

'Not the same imagination, you mean!'

An impasse settled. Thayleen noticed that the study had become very quiet. It was only by degrees that it dawned on her that the storm had ceased. The rectangle of window remained dark, with no lightning flashing against it; then, through the still undrawn curtains, she caught a glimpse of a star.

'Three violent storms in succession and rampant growth do not imply the end of the world, Mrs. West,' the Prime Minister said, rising. 'I appreciate your concern, but I am sure it is groundless. The scientists are satisfied that with the passing of the sunspot cycle all will be well.'

'Did they tell you that the spots will not pass for a hundred years?'

'Why, no — ' the Prime Minister reflected for a moment. 'However, if you will allow me to send you home in my car, I will — '

'No thank you!' Thayleen snapped, rising. 'You may be the Prime Minister, but you are an ignorant fool! I don't care whether you like the sound of that or not. As for the favour of your car, I'd sooner walk. Good *night!*'

Thayleen swung to the door, snatched it open, strode across the hall, and went out at the front doorway. When the Prime Minister reached the front steps, he could see her figure vanishing along the wet street, the emergency lighting casting sullen reflections.

'Any orders, sir?' one of the constables asked.

'Not at the moment. I — '

The Prime Minister stopped in a half-turn back into the hall. He frowned, looked hard at the top step in the dim light; and then, to make sure, he pressed the switch of his cigarette lighter and held the steady flame to the stonework.

He peered at a single blade of livid green grass. It had pushed its way through a crack in the stone, and even as he looked at it another blade came peeping through, unfurling gently and spattering drops of accumulated rain.

'That's queer, sir,' the nearest constable murmured, frowning. 'How do you suppose grass ever forced its way through the stone?'

'There must be roots underneath this step, which have smashed the stone, and the grass belongs to them. And this means — '

The Prime Minister straightened up and mused.

'Come to my study,' he said finally. 'I want you to take a message to New Bow Street immediately. Anton Drew must be released.'

The constable did not comment. He could not understand why a blade of grass had made the Prime Minister about-face. He couldn't know that to the Prime Minister it meant that one of Drew's predictions had come true. If one had then the others might. And then —

7

For Ken West, once the lightning shock had abated, there was nothing but a continuous round of searching for Thayleen. Long after the storm had ceased and a remarkable calm night had settled down, Ken was wandering blindly in various directions, hoping he would come across the girl.

Being unaware what had prompted her to dash into the storm, he had assumed it was blind panic. The idea of her going to the Prime Minister never even entered his head. For the same reason, it never occurred to him that she might return home.

In the course of the night he covered most of the surrounding countryside, calling constantly, struggling through growths that were rampantly extending, tearing himself free of monster brambles, stung by enormous nettles. He did not heed them. He had to find Thayleen — but he failed.

Towards dawn he returned home mechanically, grey as a ghost; then his emotions soared to delirious joy as he caught sight of a light in the lounge windows. He ran and stumbled over the vegetation-choked garden and through the open French windows — then he came to a halt, staring. It was not Thayleen who was there, but Anton Drew, relaxed in the armchair, his pipe smouldering.

'Forgive the liberty of an old friend walking in and sitting down,' he said, rising. Extending his hand, he added in concern: 'You look all in, man. Have a seat. Try some brandy?'

'Thanks,' Ken whispered, and fell in the nearest chair.

He took the brandy Drew gave him, and gulped it down. Then he considered Drew's unemotional features.

'I heard you were in jail, Anton. Or did I dream it?'

'I was in jail, yes. Thanks to Thayleen, I'm out of it.'

'Thayleen!' Ken jumped up and gripped the scientist's arm tightly. 'Anton, where is she? For heaven's sake, tell me! I've been searching for her ever since she went into the storm.'

'Apparently she went to the Prime Minister.'

'She — she *did*? And I thought — '

'Sit down again, Ken; you're exhausted,' Drew said. Then he continued: 'I was unexpectedly released from jail and summoned to the Prime Minister. He told me Thayleen had been to see him and pleaded with him to release me, the backbone of her plea being she was a citizen and entitled to protection from the man who could give it — me. But of course, that was not the real reason.'

'No?' Ken looked troubled.

'I think her real reason for braving the storm was not so much to gain protection for herself as for the baby which is coming. That is pure mother-instinct, of course. However, the Prime Minister wouldn't listen to her. He only changed his mind when he saw grass growing through the step of his home, a development about which I had already warned him though, of course, I was referring to cities in general. So he sent for me.'

'Where is Thayleen now?' Ken demanded.

'I don't know, old man. She left the P.M. just after the storm had ceased. I shouldn't worry too much. She probably went somewhere for the night.'

'No reason why she should when she's got a home to come to.'

Ken got up and paced restlessly. He finished prowling at the French windows and studied the grey of the dawn. It was a relief to smell a fresh wind blowing. Drew came over to him, sucking at his pipe.

'If you can concentrate for a moment,' he said, 'I've got a big assignment for you. That's why I'm here. First thing I did when I realised the P.M. was on my side was summon an extraordinary meeting of all available scientists and engineers. It didn't take long to hammer things out, since I have plans already made. It has been decided to build deep shelters to my specification, starting immediately. Other countries will make their own arrangements. Tomorrow the news will be released to the world. We have got to do that in order to get the necessary armies of workers to help us. All ordinary pursuits will cease. We have to dig like hell, or die. We're — Doomsday warriors.'

Ken said nothing.

'You'll be in charge of shelter construction,' Drew added.

'*I* will?' Ken gave a start. 'Who says so?'

'The Government. That's an order, and it's my doing. They asked me for the best available engineer to take charge and that means you. I've other things to do, figuring on how to keep a population alive underground. You and I will work constantly together, with other scientists.'

'How do you expect me to concentrate without Thayleen? Until she is with me again, or I know where she is, I can't do a thing.'

'She'll be back,' Drew said reassuringly. 'Stop fretting so much, man. My guess is she put up somewhere for the night.'

Ken nodded slowly. 'I suppose that's possible.'

'In this plan to take humanity underground, there is one thing I don't like,' Drew resumed, musing. 'Bland Enterprises will have the contract for materials.'

'What's wrong with that? Best people, surely?'

'I happen to know Mortimer Bland,' Drew replied. 'I've run across some of his products which I refused to manufacture because they were a deliberate swindle. If he tries anything like that with shelter material, heaven help us! Knowing Bland's love of money, I think he might try and make a second huge fortune out of this Government contract.'

'We'll keep tabs on him,' Ken said. 'If he tries — '

He paused, his attention taken at the same moment as Drew's by a lone figure that had appeared over the distant rise beyond the garden. A small figure, almost hidden by the flowing, waving sea of grass.

'Thay!' Ken cried, and he dashed through the open French windows, across the tangle of garden, and caught hold of the girl as she came stumbling towards him. She was streaked with blood, her clothes torn, her dark hair threshing in the fresh wind.

'I — I've been fighting,' she whispered. 'Most of the night. I — I tried to come back home, but huge insects attacked me in the fields. I — I think they were ants.'

These were all the words she uttered, then, completely worn out she collapsed. Ken picked her up and carried her into the house, thence to the bedroom. When she recovered she found herself carefully bandaged, and Ken and Drew were standing at the bedside.

'Did you say — ants?' Drew asked quietly, as Ken handed over a bowl of steaming soup. 'Ken says you had a battle with them.'

'Hardly a battle — ' Thayleen propped herself on her elbow. 'I exaggerated. They attacked me — five of them — and in trying to dodge them I had a terrible time. But they were ants! As big as Shetland ponies!'

'Which spells more trouble for us,' Drew muttered. 'Of all the insects which have been recently born to giant size, the ants are the ones I fear most. They are intelligent, utterly ruthless, and masters of organization. To the rest of our woes

I'm afraid we shall have to add major battles with termites, the sworn enemies of man.'

'Sworn enemies?' Ken repeated. 'How so?'

'Because, but for an accident of evolution, which brought man into being, the ant would be the master of Earth today. All scientists admit it. They have intelligence and the gift of reason, which no other insect has. Size alone has put them at the mercy of man. Hitherto, it has been impossible for ants to evolve into a larger size. Unlike man and other animals, the ant has no lungs — only breathing tubes. Therefore, every time the ant has tried to grow bigger, it has failed because its breathing apparatus is unable to circulate enough oxygen throughout its body. Nor could it bear its own increased weight. But suppose through cosmic ray mutation it *developed* lungs — or something akin to them — and became structurally stronger? How then? With that last barrier removed, you can imagine what will happen. I must see what can be done to deal with them until we get underground. And now I must be going — '

'Anton — ' Thayleen caught at his hand. 'I don't understand what you are doing here. I thought you were — '

'Ken will tell you everything, my dear. Now I really must hurry. See you get fit quickly.'

And with his ambiguous smile Drew went from the bedroom.

★   ★   ★

By noon the inhabitants of the changing world knew what they had to face. All normal TV programmes were stopped and, regardless of varying times in different parts of the world, Drew gave an emergency speech. And he did not conceal the danger, either.

He called for volunteer workers to report at the centers especially assigned for the purpose, and underlined an earlier government statement that all normal occupations — except for essential services — would be suspended. Every fit man, woman and child must be prepared to work to the limit.

Drew also included the armies, air forces, and navies of the world in his speech. To them he handed the task of seeking out and destroying the monster denizens of the air, land, and sea that were appearing with ever-increasing frequency. In particular the ants had to be destroyed and the termitariums located.

This job done, and the peoples of the world no longer in doubt as to what was coming, or what was required of them, Drew set to work with the engineers and foundry masters to make the first moves. Sites for the entrances to the proposed underground city were selected with great care, every fold and stratum of the bedrock itself having to be checked and analysed so as to be certain the foundations could be cast in the right 'mould'.

For many weeks, a corps of engineers and scientists beside him, Drew flew back and forth by jet plane to various parts of England — and also other countries, to check their findings — and it was during this period that the true genius of the quiet-spoken scientist with the eternally smouldering pipe became manifested. Prepared by months of previous study, there seemed to be no obstacle his nimble brain could not surmount, no moment when his habitual calm deserted him.

He took complete charge of the scientific side — with a host of scientific underlings — delegated Ken to the actual engineering work, and left it to the Governments concerned to control the ebb and flow of workers.

The first reactions to the world's end died down within a week, in which time there was a spate of suicides, crimes of violence, miniature wars, and mob law — then, as the stronger spirits took charge, the unruly ones were wiped out. Law-breakers were shot out of hand: no relaxation of ceaseless toil was permitted. For that matter, it did not take any exhortation on Drew's part to keep the workers' noses to the grindstone. A sun darkened at last by spots was sufficient goad, as were the violent storms that burst at intervals, leaving behind human beings struggling on amidst the ruins like insects that have survived the kick of a man's boot.

In the two weeks that elapsed before a start was made on the shelters, the evidences of advancing doom were obvious. It shrieked from the towering vines and alien growths which now sprouted in every city in the world — growing, swelling, crawling, fed by the radioactive soil.

It was evident again in the ceaseless onslaught of termites and giants of the insect world and animal kingdom, as armies and air forces fought against them. It was in human beings themselves with their thickened skins and strange, inexplicable diseases. It was in the dim grey sky and the frigid winds which blew through the late July days. The end had not only begun; it was well advanced.

One person who was satisfied was Mortimer Bland. The huge contract he had received from the various Governments to produce a special pressure-resisting metal made to Drew's specifications made it certain that even by honest means he would net a fortune. But by dishonest means he might get a good deal more; and for Bland the sky was always the limit. He set to work with those of his directors who were of a like mind to see what chance there was of something on the side.

In the end of the world, Bland did not believe, despite the signs. He no more doubted that the world would return to its former glory than the average man doubts but what a wet day will turn fine. There was nobody who could watch his movements — not even Milly Morton. In fact, he had completely forgotten her since she had walked out on him in Bombay.

But she had not forgotten him. Always vindictive when not obtaining all she wanted, she had never given up hope but what, somehow, somewhere, some day, she would repay Bland for the raw deal he'd handed her.

In the meantime, she had to live. So when the call came for workers, she offered herself as 'Mary Carson,' was booked down as over forty — to her secret fury — and relegated to the job of machine-minder. It was unexciting, uninteresting, yet vital work in its way. Also a worker, but in a totally different sphere, was Thayleen. She had got the better of her artistic temperament and thrown herself into the exacting task of being Ken's chief secretary. Wherever he went, she was beside him, checking his notes, keeping a record of details, and generally proving herself invaluable.

And by degrees, amidst the turmoil and distractions, progress was made. In Britain, two shafts were being made — one in the centre of Surrey, and the other in the North Midlands, which seemed to all concerned the best way of serving the northern and southern inhabitants of the British Isles. Those from Wales and Scotland would have to be transported, since there was no area in their particular countries suitable for shaft-sinking. The two shafts decided upon were to be constructed diagonally in the shape of a gigantic V, converging to give ingress to the proposed underground city. This, Drew had decided, must be at the depth of a mile.

The metal for the shaft linings that would have to be used later for the interior insulation of the huge cavern where the city itself was to be, was something Drew himself had created. Its tightly locked atomic make-up made it incredibly tough once it had left the moulds in the Bland foundries. Under pressure it remained obdurate until five million tons to the square inch was recorded; then it showed signs of bending without actual fracture. Seven million tons to the square inch seemed to be its limit, which was probably far in excess of anything it would he called upon to stand — or so Ken thought.

Drew, though, had other ideas, of which he spoke only when in solemn conclave with the high-ups.

'As we go below, gentlemen, we shall not only be fighting the ever-increasing pressure,' he said, looking around on the assembly gathered in the big underground-operations centre. 'We may also have to fight pressure from the *surface*, something which none you have taken into account.'

'How from the *surface*?' Ken asked, puzzled.

'With the increase in sunspots the sun will slowly die out, become as completely obscured as though in a perpetual total eclipse before it collapses into a white dwarf. That will mean the freezing of Earth's surface, and a glacier of imponderable weight will crush down from above. I'm taking precautions against that, hence the immense resistance of the metal we are using.'

'A glacier might destroy the vegetation and ants,' one of the scientists said. 'That would be an advantage.'

'It would also write 'Finis' to our hopes of ever returning to the surface,' Drew sighed. 'I am desperately hoping that the collapse of the sun into a nova will not take place. Given that one blessing, there is a chance that future generations taught in advance what to do, may be able to combat the wild life of the surface, once the sun returns to normal. For us, though, it is the inevitable end, because I cannot see any return to normalcy for the sun for at least a century.'

For a moment there was quietness. Each man present was scientist enough to accept the dictate of the cosmic catastrophe without flinching.

'I've been toying with an idea,' Drew said presently, a far-away look in his eyes. 'Cosmic radiation is our foe. If we could only find the source of it, we might combat it.'

'The source!' one of the scientists echoed. 'That's quite impossible, isn't it?'

'Perhaps but in our present plight I'll try anything once. I recall the Prime Minister asking me if cosmic rays could be traced to the source and destroyed, and I promptly said no. Having thought about it, I'm wondering. Cosmic rays are not uniform, and vary greatly in their intensity. Some of it can be ignored, because it is relatively weak — such as the cosmic background radiation thought to originate from the Big Bang that created the universe. The stronger sources probably spring from some stellar catastrophe originating somewhere within our own galaxy. If the strongest sources *could* be traced, we might perhaps construct a kind of spatial 'umbrella' in outer space. Sufficiently large, and constructed of highly reflective metal, such a structure, if positioned correctly, might cut off the most virulent rays from reaching the Earth . . . '

Drew shrugged. 'I'm getting ahead of myself. To even set out to find the source would demand a specially equipped spaceship, lead-sheathed to protect the pilot from the increase in solar flares, and cosmic radiation. As you know, the crew of the international space station have had to be evacuated, and currently all spacecraft are grounded, along with high-flying planes . . . Forget it gentlemen; I get beyond myself sometimes,'

But Drew kept the idea at the back of his mind just the same. In the meantime, he had much to do. And the work went on.

As the lower depths of the shafts were reached, those engaged upon them — numbering several thousands — felt a good deal happier and better spirited than for month's past. It seemed a strange reaction when they were digging for their lives, but for the scientists it had an explanation. It meant that the lower man went, the less cosmic radiation could affect him, and the more normal became his physique and mentality. Many, indeed, began to lose the curious thickening of skin that had come to most men and women, and they began to look as they had before the Blight, as the catastrophe was now popularly called.

For Anton Drew, usually working close to the surface, no such restoration to normal occurred. In energy he was undimmed; in ideas he seemed more brilliant than ever, but there was no denying the increased greyness of his hair, and the coarseness of his exposed flesh.

At intervals the workers caught glimpses of Mortimer Bland as he came to survey a section under construction. So far, he had not attempted any monkey business. He had decided to wait for the time when the testing engineers would be less vigilant, when crisis was so urgent that they would assume all consignments were as good as each other.

Once Milly Morton saw Bland from a distance. Her thick hands tightened on the controls of the small mechanical excavator she was operating.

'What's the matter?' asked the man worker with her, noticing her convulsive action and intense stare. 'Don't you like the look of old man Bland?'

'I hate the dirty beast!' Milly whispered.

Barry Johnson, her fellow operator, shrugged. He was a big, powerfully built man of thirty, an ex-stratosphere pilot, and assigned to the task of shoveling and pick-axeing where no machine could operate. Between them, he and Milly — with thousands of others — were clearing a predetermined section.

'Bland and I were once like that, Barry,' Milly added, and held up two interlocking fingers.

'You were?' Barry looked doubtful.

'I know what you're thinking — that Bland wouldn't have anything to do with a has-been like me. That's just it! When I started to look like this he threw me out.

Before that, I had everything. Ever hear of Milly Morton, the musical comedy star?'

'In the days before the Blight? Sure thing. I saw her on the stage many a time — then she disappeared.'

'I'm she,' Milly said dryly. 'And I don't blame you for not believing it.'

'I don't,' Barry grinned, and returned to his work.

But in the passage of several more days, Barry had reason to think again on Milly's assertion. As he and Milly were transferred to the lower depths of the shaft, some 800 feet below their former level, they began to experience the same slow and baffling recovery from cosmic radiation effects as those already domiciled in these depths.

Of necessity, neither Milly, Barry Johnson, nor any of the workers on this particular drilling section were allowed to leave the site of operations. In their off-time they read, played cards, talked, arranged amateur theatricals and parties amongst themselves, and generally lived as any small community might in an exploration of some remote part of the world.

Thuswise, cut off from fifty per cent of the radiation existing at higher levels, Milly began to change — for the better. First, she lost weight, which pleased her considerably; then she gradually realised that the spurious flesh and ugliness she had gained though excessive cell-accruement was also breaking down. Barry Johnson, himself changing from a thick-necked plug-ugly into quite a handsome, clean-cut man, became increasingly interested — and bewildered — by the gradual metamorphosis of a middle-aged dowager into a slim and lovely young woman. After two weeks at the lower level, Milly said again that she was Milly Morton — and Barry Johnson didn't doubt it.

'Ever think of getting married?' he asked her.

'Sometimes. I never seem to find the right kind of man.'

'What kind of man do you expect?'

'Oh, somebody famous. Like Bland, for instance. Or maybe a public figure, a hero, or something. I like you a lot, Barry, but you haven't much to your name, have you? Never done anything big, I mean?'

''Fraid I haven't,' Barry reflected. 'I may do one day. If I did, Milly, do you think you — '

'I might,' Milly said, and left it at that.

8

Lower and lower still went the shafts
— 700-feet, 1,000-feet, 1,500-feet, the
walls lined with almost seamless curved
plates of the special Drew metal, whilst
behind them was a further lining of dense
material of asbestos-like quality, and
behind that again was lead, 2-feet thick.
Drew was convinced that with such
protection and a maximum depth of
5,280-feet for the proposed city — one
mile below — mankind would be isolated
from cosmic radiation and able to
function more or less normally.

He was already cheered by the news of
the recovery of radiation victims at the
lower depths, and wherever possible
expectant mothers were sent to these
regions.

Thayleen was one of the first to go
below, and to prevent any suggestion of
favouritism Ken went too, the ramifica-
tions of his work as chief engineer

demanding his presence lower down.

News of the outer world was fragmentary. Intercontinental air travel had ceased because of the dangers to crew and passengers from cosmic radiation and, more recently, solar flares. Additionally, those in authority could not see any good purpose could be served by reporting on cities crumbling under mad vegetation; of giant insects swarming amidst the jungles and choking the skies and oceans; of a sun blotched and unreal and dimmed to moonlight glow even at high noon; of a deadly drop in temperature the world over; and the formation of ice in temperate waters and spreading of the polar caps.

There was no longer a doubt that the hand of death was tightening on the world, and it was still in the balance whether the crisis would pass and leave the sun able to struggle back to its former grandeur, or whether —

Drew, to whom came all reports, pushed the alternative on one side as too appalling to contemplate. He went on with his plans for the underground city, in touch with Governments by radio throughout the world as they too, using every available citizen, burrowed down and down, defeating volcanic seams, overcoming subsidences, somehow maintaining a constant food supply, partly natural — from accumulated stocks — and partly synthetic from mobile laboratories.

For the world's various Governments to use every soul was impossible. Through invalidism or other reasons thousands had to be rejected. These became the Unfortunates, as they were called. They were ruthlessly shut out by mighty metal valves, which sealed the shafts from the outer world.

Once the fury and resentment of the Unfortunates had spent itself they were left to fend for themselves. They fought each other for what food there was; they struggled against the monster beasts and insects and choking vegetation around them; they coarsened and devolved under the drenching cosmic radiation from a sky dimmed to twilight — and at last they died, a forgotten legion of the Doomsday warriors.

Two thousand feet, 2,500-feet and going became slower. Bland moved his blast furnaces and equipment and foundries to lower regions and kept up the constant stream of materials. So far, everything was going perfectly, but the struggle against lower pressures was becoming tougher. Several of the huge atomic-driven drills snapped against the harder rock and had to be re-designed. The hold-ups made the engineers in charge dance with chagrin.

By this time August had become September. September and October went, and in the floodlit depths nobody knew the difference. They all lived in an eternal clangour of vast machines, the whine and grind of drills, the rattle of shovels and picks, the smell of hot oil and exhaust fumes. Never in his varied career on Earth had Man worked with such unceasing endeavour or with such high courage.

By the time the 3,000-foot depth was reached the various testing engineers were so busy examining the new drills and planning fresh equipment they had little time for anything else. Bland was quite aware of it and went into action.

The first slightly adulterated plates went into position at the 3,000-foot level, becoming progressively divorced from the original formula as time went on, until Bland was satisfied that fifty per cent of the money he was receiving from Government grant was more or less clear profit. The fact that he might never be able to spend the money never occurred to him. He was making it, and old habits die hard.

About this time, Thayleen retired from her secretarial duties pending the arrival of her baby in the huge mobile hospital section specially devised for the use of workers. The woman in Thayleen's place was coldly efficient, but she lacked the fire of interest that Ken found so stimulating.

'I've been wondering about something, Anton,' Ken said on one of the occasions when he and Drew held a conference. 'When we finally join the two shafts into the central cavern where we'll build the city, does it mean we'll shut ourselves off from all contact with the outer world? If so, how are we to know if — and when — the surface becomes habitable?'

'The shafts will be our means of contacting the surface,' Drew replied. 'At the moment, each shaft — like those in other countries — is covered with a metal shield. That is a makeshift. Later, a small dome will be constructed, small so that there will be less surface area to resist the pressure of a glacier if one forms. I have worked out its composition. It will be transparent and will have a polarised atomic make-up, which is the most efficient method of blocking cosmic radiation, in glass anyway. These domes, one for each shaft, will be used as observation posts, and for brief spells at a time — brief so as to avoid the radiation which will seep even through *that* glass — we can take readings of Earth and heaven. The dome will also be made to slide on one side so exploration of the surface can be made, or if necessary a projectile can be fired into space.'

'What projectile?' Ken asked in surprise.

Drew smiled. 'I haven't yet given up my idea of trying to find the source of the most destructive cosmic rays.' He did not enlarge on the subject, however, but kept to the matter on hand. 'Once we have ploughed down the last two thousand feet we'll have the tough job of creating the enormous inner cavern. We've chosen a point rich in mineral and ore deposit. Coal, iron, oil and other necessities should be at this depth in the city-site for the asking. I have also arranged for adequate lighting, approaching daylight as much as possible — '

'What about ultra violet?' Ken asked. 'It's a vital solar commodity, and we're not getting it down here.'

'We shall when the city is erected. I have made provision for that, and breathable atmosphere. It will be as it is now, created by the heating of barium-oxide — which we have in unlimited quantity — with dehydrated soda lime and calcium chloride to remove carbonic acid. Then of course the plants we'll grow will add their quota to keeping the air sweet.'

Drew reflected for a moment.

'Water is simple,' he continued. 'As we have travelled down we have also carried with us a piping system by which the oceans themselves will supply us after filterisation through special plants. Even if the oceans freeze we'll not be defeated; it will simply be a matter of thawing. As for food, all the available canned supplies of the country are in our 'frig plants and will be rationed out until we see how things go. We have a smaller community to feed than before. We shall grow wheat, barley, fruit trees and grass. In fact I have only one regret . . . '

'What?' Ken inquired, and Drew held up his pipe.

'I'll have to stop smoking. In limited air supply it just won't do. Take it with the rest of the hardships — '

His sentence was drowned out by the sudden buzzing of the alarm signal on the wall. He swung to it in surprise as at the same moment, from outside the headquarters, there came the distant ringing of a bell and the sharp blasting of an electric hooter.

'Accident!' Ken exclaimed, leaping up. 'Come on!'

He raced from the room. Drew picked up the telephone connecting him with the operations site.

'What's gone wrong?' he asked quickly.

'Bad cave-in, Mr. Drew. Started about a hundred feet above us and part of the shaft has come down. It's buried some of the department stores and most of the hospital section.'

'I'll be there,' Drew said tautly, and switching off he raced to the door. In the space of a few minutes he had caught up with Ken and the hurrying scientists and engineers. It was only a matter of moments before they reached the chaos where the collapse had occurred.

Men and women, grimy and struggling, were crawling like flies over mountains of buckled metal sheets and fallen rock. The blazing lights picked them out in sharp detail as they worked desperately to clear away the debris.

'It's the hospital section!' Ken cried, swinging round on Drew in horror, 'My God, Thayleen — '

149

He flung himself into the struggle to try and remove the accumulated tons of rock and metal. Drew took his gaze from the frantic scene and turned to one of the engineers.

'What the devil's happened?' he demanded. 'Those plates should never have given way if they'd been properly fixed — and according to my reports they were.'

The engineer rubbed a hand over his greasy face and looked above him. He pointed to where a monstrous rent was gaping in the otherwise smooth metal interior of the shaft. Two other sections of plate that had not so far fallen were hanging perilously.

'Get up there quickly,' Drew ordered. 'Get those plates fixed and repair the breach as fast as you can. As for these plates that have fallen I want them analysed as quickly as possible. I'll attend to that personally. Go on — hurry!'

The engineer nodded and shouted to his army of workers, bawling directions at them. Drew turned and lent his assistance to the task of clearing away the ruins of the hospital section. He, Ken, and every available worker worked for three hours non-stop before they succeeded in getting to those who had been buried. Then began the accounting, the roll call, the procession of battered bodies on stretchers being removed from the ruins.

For hours afterwards Ken sat almost motionless on the old couch in Drew's private headquarters, staring immovably in front of him. Drew said nothing, assured from long friendship that his silence would not be mistaken for indifference.

'I — I can't believe it, Anton,' Ken whispered at last. 'I just *can't*! That — that Thay is dead! That the mangled body we dragged out was — '

'I'm afraid it was Thayleen,' Drew said quietly. 'The fingerprints checked.'

Ken rubbed his forehead bemusedly. Drew took out his pipe, looked at it, then with a sigh put it unlighted between his teeth.

'Ken, there is something you should know,' he said at length. 'It may help you to bear Thayleen's death more easily.'

'Nothing can make me do that.'

'You may be mistaken, old man. I don't wish to sound callous, but perhaps it is better Thayleen died when she did, than later.'

'What the hell do you mean?' Ken sprang up, his eyes hard.

'I'm talking about the baby which was expected. Had it been born it would not have been a child in the normal sense; it would have been a hideous freak, a travesty of a human being, one of the first in a new race of monsters that are going to grow up amongst us unless we destroy them. I think the shock, granting she didn't die in childbirth, would have killed a gentle soul like Thayleen.'

'You're crazy!' Ken grated.

'No.' Drew shook his untidy head. 'I have known for some months, from the X-ray plates which were taken from time to time through the medical service, what kind of a child Thayleen was going to have — if any. That was one reason why I rushed her to these lower depths as fast as possible. Also, the terrible nervous shocks she got during those storms did not improve things . . . I've been racking my

152

brains to try and think of a way to explain things gently. Now I don't have to bother.'

'I shall never know,' Ken said slowly, 'whether you are telling me this to make me more resigned to what has happened, or whether it is the truth.'

'It is the truth, as you'll see when others are born.'

Ken sat down again. Drew sat beside him. He took his pipe from his teeth and played with it in his strong hands. 'She's better dead, Ken,' he said at last. 'Better off than we are. I'm speaking off the cuff for a moment. Our outlook is pretty grim. Locked down here in this blasted tomb until we die, creeping about in artificial light, never seeing again the beauty of a summer day, never feeling the soft breath of the wind, never smelling the sweetness of the earth when rain has passed. We shall stand it, because we have to — but what would it have meant for Thayleen? It would have crushed her down, as it will crush all those who are not strong enough to survive.'

Ken got on his feet again, only his eyes

revealing the naked hurt he had received.

'I believe,' he said deliberately, 'that Thay was *murdered*! It would never have happened but for that shaft lining giving way. Not only she was murdered, but others too.'

'A hundred and thirty seven men and women died,' Drew said colourlessly, looking at the roll call on the table.

'I personally supervised the construction of that shaft lining,' Ken continued fiercely. 'Not by one iota did I diverge from the plan we'd made. There are only two answers — a sudden collapse of bedrock through volcanic action, which strikes me as pretty unlikely; or else faulty manufacture in the plates themselves. Don't forget who's back of them — Mortimer Bland. You said at the start he might pull something.'

'I know,' Drew admitted. 'I'll be better able to judge when the analysts have been to work. And if Bland has been up to some funny business he'll have to explain it to our court.'

'To hell with that! If he's at all guilty I'm going to kill him myself, Anton! If I die because of murdering him it doesn't signify. I've nothing to live for, anyway.'

Drew did not argue there and then. He knew the strain under which Ken was labouring. Instead he said: 'We have unpleasant work to perform. Mass burial service for the victims of the disaster. You'll have to be present, Ken, harrowing though it will be.'

★   ★   ★

In six hours, all boring operations suspended for the time being as a token of respect for those who had been buried, the testing experts had completed their findings.

At an extraordinary meeting in Drew's headquarters he sat grimly awaiting the result.

'The metal is faulty, Mr. Drew,' the chief testing engineer said, tossing a small fragment of it on the desk under the bright light. 'But whether the fault lies with Bland or the human element it's hard to say.'

'Not to me it isn't,' Ken remarked acidly.

155

Drew picked up the metal and turned it in his fingers.

'What's all this pitting and scarring on one side of it?' he asked.

'Air bubbles. They arise in metals at times during the smelting, of course and with this kind of metal especially because ordinary smelting processes are not used. My guess is that the metal developed air bubbles throughout its structure which made it weak.'

'What does the analysis chart show?'

'Seventy five percent formula metal; fifteen adulteration. That can be accounted for by impurities being sucked into the metal during the smelting.'

'And it happened with all the plates concerned in the collapse?'

The testing engineer nodded. 'Three plates gave way. The two which almost did — and which are now back in position — have normal readings and apparently no faults. So have those immediately below the gap. We've had ultrasonic detectors over them, and they don't reveal any bubble flaws.'

'If you ask me,' Ken said grimly,

156

'Mortimer Bland is slipping faulty metal amongst the good, it being as difficult to find as the needle in the haystack, especially at the high speed we're working at. He knows damned well we've too much on at the moment to be checking every little square inch of the stuff.'

'To range over three thousand feet of shaft and check every plate is impossible!' the engineer protested.

'In this instance,' Drew said, 'we cannot act against Bland. We still have laws, even down here, and he'd work the benefit-of-the-doubt angle. It *could* be faulty smelting due to hurry; it *could* be extreme volcanic pressure from the rocks that tore the shaft at its weakest point. We have just got to let it go, but if we come across one plate hereafter which is wrong, then Bland will be called to account.'

He rose to his feet. 'That's all, boys, thanks.'

Ken watched the men go and then he swung to Drew.

'You may be letting Bland get away with it, Anton, but you've reckoned without me!' He jumped to his feet. 'I

157

told you what I'd do if I had reasonable grounds for thinking he caused the disaster which killed Thay.'

'Yes I know. You said you'd kill him. Go ahead. I fully believe that he caused the disaster, but I can't prove it. As for you, what satisfaction do you get from killing him, beyond the brief seconds when you do it?'

'I'll be avenging Thay. That's enough for me.'

Ken swung to the door; then Drew's quiet voice halted him. 'Ken, do you think Thayleen would have agreed to you murdering Bland? Two blacks don't make a white, you know.'

'I'm going just the same.'

'Have it your own way.'

Ken went. Closing the door emphatically. Drew turned back to a study of the metal fragment. Perhaps ten minutes later he glanced up as Ken came back into the office. His white-faced fury seemed to have cooled somewhat.

'Perhaps — perhaps you are right, Anton,' he said, musing. 'To oneself be true, I suppose. If Thay should be watching me, I wouldn't like her to think that I — '

'Sit down,' Drew suggested quietly. 'I want to discuss some new borings with you. And don't bother your head over Bland. If he's the double-crosser we think he'll get it handed back, in a way we'd never be able to foresee.'

9

Towards the end of the 'day', marked by the chronometer, Drew had a caller in Barry Johnson. He was still in the soiled overalls of his shift, his face grease-smudged and dirty.

Drew looked at him expectantly.

'Sorry to interrupt you like this, Mr. Drew,' Barry Johnson apologised, 'but I've been hearing one or two things about a theory you're working on, and I thought I might be able to help.'

'What theory?' Drew asked in surprise.

'I've heard you are trying to find the source of cosmic radiation with a view to learning all about it, and then if possible negating its influence.'

'That's true enough, but who told you?'

'General rumour, sir. Things get about. It was the girl I work with — Milly Morton — who told me.'

'Mmm. Did you say Milly Morton?'

'Yes, sir. That's her real name. She's

registered as Mary Carson. She's my machine mate. I'm Barry Johnson and we're working together on Excavation 27.'

Drew nodded, thinking of all Milly Morton stood for.

'It occurred to me,' Barry went on, 'that if you are looking for a pilot for a space projectile — and I gather you are — I might be able to do the job. I'm an ex-stratosphere jet flyer and accustomed to the strains. Given the chance I might discover all you want.'

'You realise, Mr. Johnson, that the chances of death or madness are very high?'

'Yes, sir.' The young man nodded without flinching. 'I don't mind that, though. I've risked my neck more times than I can remember. Besides, I don't like being pinned down here. If I've got to die I'd sooner do it under the sky, however changed it might be. It also seems to me there's no better way to die than helping one's fellows.'

'Very praiseworthy,' Drew commented. 'And that is the main reason for your — er — generous offer?'

Barry grinned a little. 'Let's say part of it, sir. The main reason is Milly. I'm — I'm pretty much that way about her, but she's a girl with decided ideas on the kind of man she wants to marry. He's either got to have wealth — which is hopeless for me as things are — or else be publicly acclaimed, or something. I can't think of any way to achieve that except perhaps by making this discovery you want. If I die, okay. I shan't be able to worry then, anyway. But if I should come back with information which might save the human race — Well, Milly couldn't want more than that, could she?'

'You wouldn't think so,' Drew replied ambiguously. 'So she put you up to this idea, did she?'

'That's right, sir.'

Drew said no more about Milly — he knew the young man would never accept it. Instead he turned to the actual subject.

'My plans are sufficiently advanced for a test flight to be made,' he said. 'The test will not at first be to find cosmic rays, but to see if space travel works.'

'I can't think why it shouldn't,' Barry said earnestly.

'There is one possible snag,' Drew warned. 'Man has accepted that space can be crossed, but has not paid much attention to how devastating cosmic radiation can be. He has found that out since it started raining down on Earth. It has taught me that all the old theories for protection against cosmic radiation in space are outmoded. Very special shielding is needed, chiefly that of lead — which unfortunately retards the initial take-off speed of the projectile — and a spaceship metal itself utilizing an atomic make-up which is polarised, thereby limiting the passage of radiation through its interstices to the absolute minimum.'

'I leave those technical details to you, sir,' Barry said. 'All I'm doing is offering myself.'

'And I appreciate it. The moment I have something definitely settled — as I will have — I'll get in touch with you.'

'I'll be here,' Barry promised, and left the office.

Drew pondered for a while, trying to

think of some possible reason for Milly suggesting that the young man should risk almost certain death. Drew was perfectly sure, from what he had seen of Milly, that she would never keep her word and marry Barry even if he did acquit himself heroically — so there must be some other motive.

But Drew had no time to weigh up the machinations of Milly Morton. All that interested him was that he had found a volunteer for the hazardous task of testing space, so in every available moment he pushed on with the design of a space projectile.

In the meantime other operations continued. A further 1,000-feet was bored, at the cost of a dozen broken drills and several lives. Only 1,000-feet now remained before the cavern hollowing could begin. Ken at least was glad of the work; it made it easier for him to go on living.

One uneasy person was Mortimer Bland. He had expected his spurious metal to stand up for many years before its adulterated composition gave way

— years in which he hoped for a return to the surface whereby his double-crossing would never be discovered.

The destruction of the hospital and so many lives scared him. He gave orders for all future metal to be hundred per cent pure — but then he had uncomfortable thoughts about the thousands of metal plates being used every hour, of which only fifty per cent were really perfect. Bland could not quite understand why he had escaped interrogation after the hospital disaster. He felt as if he were living on the edge of a volcano.

Then, one 'evening', a little while after the public announcement that Barry Johnson was going to make an attempt to re-conquer space — with a view to locating cosmic ray sources — Milly Morton appeared in Bland's office at the 4,000-foot level.

For a quarter of a minute, Bland sat staring at her fixedly, as she stood beside his desk. She was smiling, beautiful, and altogether desirable. Before coming she had taken pains to dress herself in the finest clothes the underworld could offer, and delicately applied make-up enhanced every line of her features.

'Surprised, Mort?' she asked softly, and though she gave no sign of it she was studying him. He had lost his former coarseness, she noticed.

'Surprised!' he echoed. 'I'd forgotten all about you.'

'I have never forgotten you,' Milly half leaned over the desk, wafting a seductive perfume. 'I made up my mind that when I had the chance I'd look you up again. So here I am — the original Milly Morton, willing to bury the hatchet and forget that awful business that turned me into a hag and you into a prize pig.'

Bland grinned and got up to pull forth a chair for her.

'That cosmic radiation did make a mess of us,' he agreed. 'Well, what sort of work are you doing now?'

'I'm on an excavator. It isn't exciting, but I get by.'

'I can always add a secretary.'

'Not again, Mort. Drew has too much authority these days for that. He'd throw me out. Incidentally, he wasn't far wrong in his prediction, was he? The Blight is here — to stay.'

'For a while, yes,' Bland admitted. 'But I haven't given up hope that in a year or two we'll be back above. In the meantime I'm making more money than I ever dreamed possible, turning out metal for the shafts.'

'You ought to, considering the metal you're using,' Milly commented drily. 'I was once your secretary, remember, and I learned then that many of your deals were not quite — er — I've no reason to think you'd changed. I'd be disappointed in you if you did.'

'You would?' Bland gave his broad grin.

'I like men who gain power by taking chances: you know that. It is generally admitted that the plates which caused the hospital disaster were 'doctored', but most of the workers have their doubts. So this time you got away with it. But you won't again, Mort. I'm warning you.'

'The plates *were* faulty,' Bland admitted. 'But it was none of my doing. A laboratory error; you know how it is. My worry is that there may be other plates like those . . . '

'I rather thought something like that might be troubling you,' Milly said, after a pause. 'So I decided to look you up and make a suggestion. Suppose you could get away from this shelter business altogether — would it make you happier?'

'It would take a load off my mind; but what are you talking about? We can't get away from here. We're sealed in.'

'One person isn't — that young chap Barry Johnson who's going to venture into space to see if it can be done in a specially-shielded vessel. Suppose his mission is a success? That will mean he is not the only person who can leave Earth.'

A bright look came into Bland's prominent eyes.

'You mean that I — or rather we — could escape into space?'

'Why not?'

'But I'd planned to be a commercial giant on the surface when all this is over — '

'Where's the guarantee it ever will be?' Milly demanded. 'I think we're down here

168

for keeps, Mort! And you may get entangled when more plates give way. If we can get out, then let's go . . . Think! We could cruise through infinity for the rest of our lives. At least we'd die in the infinite and not in a tomb like this. Wouldn't you rather die amidst the stars than down here in this stink of oil and human beings?'

'Perhaps — I would,' Bland admitted, after some thought. 'I just don't like the thought of throwing away the possible chance to become world dictator later on.'

'If you stay here and there's another collapse you'll get a lethal chamber,' Milly retorted. 'And you know it!'

Bland gave a gloomy nod; then presently he brightened up again.

'Yes, it's a good notion, Milly. I could pay the engineers who have constructed the test vessel to build me a machine on the same principle. Secretly, I mean. My own foundries could turn out a small space machine, fitted with every possible comfort, designed for two people — '

Milly nodded slowly.

169

'The problem would be to get Drew to open up the shaft for us to depart,' Bland added, pondering.

'That might not be so difficult. I've looked into that part of the business myself. Drew gives the orders, of course, and the shaft is only opened when he says so — one or the other that is. But he doesn't do the actual job himself. That is up to the powerhouse engineers who have charge of lighting, radio communication and so forth. I think that with some of that precious money of yours it shouldn't be hard to bribe the engineer concerned to open the shaft for us for the brief time necessary to make a dash for it.'

'We'd be seen departing.'

'Would it matter? With only one other space flyer in commission — the test projectile — do you suppose Drew would waste time chasing us? Probably he'd be glad to see the back of us: he doesn't exactly love either of us.'

'He wouldn't let me go that easily,' Bland said. 'I have too much power and influence on the production side. As long as I seem to be playing the game straight he'll hold me here, if he can.'

'For what? To turn out his precious plates and build a city for a lot of brainless fools who'll stay down here until they rot. What do we care about them?'

Bland brought the flat of his hand down on the desk.

'You've suggested the neatest way ever of side-stepping responsibilities,' he said. 'If space *is* navigable it opens up a way of escaping possible retribution down here. But it might become monotonous after a while.'

'No more so than being down here.'

Bland reached across and patted Milly's slender hand.

'Okay, Milly, we'll run it your way. Just let that fellow Johnson come back safely and I'll fix the rest. If he doesn't — well, we'll have to think again, eh?'

'Of course.' Milly rose from her chair. 'Which seems to be all for now. Whenever I can see you, I will, but you know there isn't much time in this pest-hole. 'Bye for now.'

'Don't I rate a kiss?' Bland demanded, standing beside her.

'Be plenty of time for that later, won't there?' she asked, and evading his clumsy movement towards her, she left the office.

★   ★   ★

Practically everybody in the southern shaft was present to watch Barry Johnson make his journey into space. It was three 'days' after Milly had visited Mortimer Bland that Barry lay sealed in his lead-sheathed cocoon, stretched full length, the controls so placed that they were within easy reach of his hands, with the observation window a foot from his face. Everything that Drew could conceive to block cosmic radiation and solar flares had been incorporated into the projectile, and because of its weight with so much lead and heavy interlocking structure in its make-up, the projectile had only room for a single pilot.

The motive power was atomic force controlling two single recoiling rockets in the tail of the machine, with three subsidiary rockets at the sides for left-right movement and braking.

Barry himself was quite confident that his suicide plunge would succeed. Through the windows of the projectile — it being tilted to 45 degrees so as to be in a directly parallel line with the shaft leading to the surface — he could see the gathered people watching interestedly, all of them at a distance, so that the fiery blast of the rockets when he opened them up at a radio command would not strike them.

Drew himself was on a specially made control platform a quarter of a mile distant. With him were Ken and members of the Government, together with scientists and engineers. Not that Barry cared about them: he was mainly concerned in whether or not Milly was watching. Even if not, he remained satisfied that when he returned from the trip all opposition to marrying him would surely have been swept away.

'You there, Barry?' came Drew's voice through the loudspeaker.

'Yes, sir, and everything's okay.' Barry came to attention at the voice.

'Now, you know what to do. You'll build up power to the limit of what you can physically stand to give yourself the initial take-off. If anything should go wrong, our instruments will reveal it. The removal of your hands from the power controls will break a photo-electric cell radio circuit. We can then bring the projectile back by remote control. If all goes well, report to me by radio short wave as you travel. Your communications will probably be blurred by static, but we'll sort it.'

'Right, sir.'

'That's all. Off you go — and good luck.'

Barry closed his hand over the power control switch. For a brief moment he hesitated; then he shifted the lever into the first notch. In the tail of the projectile the rockets burst and roared into life as the energy fired them. Another notch and the rocket-projectile took off with the lightness of a bird. Already predetermined for its line of flight, it swept smoothly into the gaping maw of the shaft.

His eyes fixed ahead, Barry watched the walls flying soundlessly past him, apparently horizontal instead of vertical.

Faster and faster still, until a dim spot grew swiftly into a circle studded with stars.

The stars paled as the area of the circle increased — then suddenly the projectile had flashed out of the open shaft top and into the atmosphere. It was day — late afternoon to judge from the position of the sun — and as he fled from the incredibly changed world, Barry looked about him.

All sight or sign of cities seemed to have disappeared. There was a crawling, endless jungle of fantastic bile-green plants towering to an incredible height, which effectually hid everything at ground level. There was no longer any doubt but what Earth had returned to a stage approximating that of the Carboniferous Era.

Turning slightly, Barry peered at the sun. It was not painful to do so. He could gaze on it without wincing, surveying the reddish disk with its yawning sunspot caverns. Three-quarters of the face was obscured by them: the remainder had lost its blinding brilliance and seemed as though it shone through a blanketing mist of cold vapours.

In general, the sky was clear at the moment, though to the far East there was the flickering of an electric storm. Then, as he travelled higher, Barry caught a glimpse of where the Atlantic and English Channel had been. They were partly ice-covered and the remainder choked with vegetation. It seemed odd to him that luxurious vegetation could exist side by side with ice; then it dawned on him that the plants below were not natural plants but by-products of isotope-impregnated soil, plants adapted to stand the deathly chill that was on the world.

All this information he presently radioed back to Earth, and Drew's voice floated to him in response, by no means clear, owing to the perpetual electronic interference of sunspots.

'We're closing the shaft-top until you give the signal that you are returning, Barry,' Drew said. 'We can't risk allowing any of that vegetation to take root in the shaft, or of allowing our air pressure to fall too much. You say the sun is still surviving?'

'Seems to be, sir, but it's blotchy and red.'

'You have instruments aboard to make tests. Get a bolometer reading of the solar surface and all possible visual recordings with the telephoto lens. Also photograph Earth itself as you see it from above. The information will be valuable later. And also test the cosmic-ray strength with those Geiger counters you have.'

'Right, sir.'

Fully trained to the task he was now undertaking, Barry turned to work, and for the next half-hour he was busy with all the instruments concerned. By the time he had finished, the instruments showed him that he had travelled a considerable distance from Earth and was heading towards the pale shadow of the Moon at an almost constant velocity. He cut down the rocket power until it was just sufficient to keep him out of the backward drag of Earth's mass, and reported once more to Drew. This time he could hardly hear, or be heard, so severe was interference.

'Keep — news — for later,' Drew's distorted voice ordered. 'Only communicate — when near Earth again.'

Barry switched off and lay contemplating space. He had had near glimpses of it before in his stratosphere trips but this was the first time he had ever floated in the free void with the hosts of heaven around him. It was fascinating and yet frightening at the same time — depthless distance spread upon distance, the stars blazing with a steady, unwavering brightness now there was no air to mask them.

Mars, Venus, Saturn, Mercury — he picked them out with difficulty, owing to their albedos being so low with the sun's light diminished; then he came back to looking at the sun itself. The corona was pale and the writhing prominences mere flickers, compared to what he had expected. Though his knowledge of the sun was not profound, he had imagination enough to realise that the orb of day was on its last legs unless some radical change took place in its constitution.

Then something else took his attention.

It was something both horrifying yet uncannily interesting. His hands were commencing to grow a thick crop of hair on the backs! Astonished, he lay watching his hands as they held the switches — and with a staggering speed they changed from the hands of a man to the paws of an ape!

Barry could hardly feel the transformation beyond a faint tingling of the skin. When he could feel it about his face and body, real fear got him. He snatched down the small mirror from the side wall and propped it in front of him.

He was not looking into his own face but that of a hideous ape. In a matter of minutes, as it seemed, unguessable ages of evolution had gone for nothing, and he had reverted to the primordial ancestor from which he had sprung.

The mirror dropped out of his hand and splintered on the floor. He had no idea what he was doing here, holding switches and flying through space. The chief anxiety in his mind was to find trees, a tribe, a mate, and food. He was desperately hungry. He growled angrily to himself and stirred as he lay on his stomach — then he looked uncomprehendingly at the loudspeaker as, crackling violently it came to life.

'Barry — is everything — all right?' came Drew's wavering voice. 'This is just a check-up.'

The ape that had been Barry Johnson stared fixedly. And back on Earth, Drew waited anxiously beside the radio apparatus, frowning at his colleagues as no answer came forth.

'Either static has drowned him out or there's something very much wrong,' Ken said, and the other men nodded.

'I can hear something,' Drew said suddenly, now listening with headphones instead of the speaker. 'A sort of growling — just like an animal. Here — listen.'

Ken took the phones from him, concentrated, nodded, and then handed them on. Drew turned to the meters and examined them. He gave a start as he saw that the photo-electric cell indicator was pointing to zero.

'Something queer!' he exclaimed. 'Both his hands are away from the switches

— contrary to orders. We daren't risk any more,' he broke off. 'It's over ten thousand miles away and still going, but if that projectile is out of control, anything can happen. Better start bringing him back.'

The chief radio engineer nodded and went to work on the remote-control apparatus. Drew looked about him on the people gathered nearby. Though they were not actually awaiting Barry's return, they were anxious for news.

'If anything has gone wrong, we can't afford to plunge these folks into despair,' Drew murmured to Ken, standing beside him. So, raising his voice, he added: 'There's no good purpose to be served, folks, by you standing around here waiting for something to happen. As far as we can tell at the minute, everything is according to plan. In the meantime, normal work on the boring is being held up. You'd better get back to work. The moment anything happens you'll be informed.'

This, coming from Drew, was as good as an order; so the men and women

— Milly Morton amongst them, and Bland at a distance — broke up and began to return to their various tasks. Drew watched them disperse, and then turned to the radio engineer.

'How's it coming, Bob?'

'Okay. We've got the projectile under control and have cut off the rockets by radio impulses. We can start the forward rockets going as soon as we get the projectile nearer to Earth, then we can brake its fall. Doesn't look too good, Mr. Drew. Young Johnson must have passed out or something — '

'Not altogether,' Ken said, studying the photo-electric reaction reading. 'Every now and again he takes hold of the switches and then lets go again.'

Drew also pondered the instrument, then shrugged.

'I've not the least idea what he's playing at. Anyway, the machine is out of his control now, so it doesn't matter much what he does.'

'It might be a good idea,' Ken said, 'if we went up to the surface and had a look when he lands. It will be difficult to get the projectile down here by radio control; and also, if there is anything serious — like Johnson being badly burned or something — we don't want anybody to see it. Too depressing.'

Drew nodded. 'Good enough. You and I can go up to the surface and leave these chaps here with the controls.'

He gave directions to the engineers, explained matters to the others in the group, and then he and Ken took the elevator to the summit of the shaft. Here they turned into the storage cavern, where there were kept the protective suits for use on the surface. So far, they had not been used; but Drew was taking no chances in risking the outer world without adequate protection against radiation and cold.

In five minutes he and Ken were dressed like divers, and began to climb up the twisting metal ladder that led to the underside of the shaft cover. Pressure on a button was sufficient signal to below to cause the massive metal lid to slide back slightly in its grooves. The two men continued up the ladder and walked over the mighty metal lip to the outdoors.

'What about having it closed again?' Ken asked through the linked audio-phone.

'No need for the moment. That small segment won't cause much air-pressure leakage.' Drew looked about him through his face-visor, and Ken heard him whistle softly in the audiophone. 'Sweet hell, did you ever see anything like that?' he asked.

Ken never had, and said so. Vegetation was towering infinitely far above their heads, blotting out the blue-violet sky. Here and there between gargantuan leaves and branches, they had a glimpse of cold, star-dusted sky. The sun itself was too low towards the horizon for visibility with so much intervening jungle. Both men found it impossible to realize that this was the clear, sandy valley floor in which the shaft had been sunk six months before. In the interval, a forest of Amazonian dimensions had sprung up — and, as they shortly discovered, it was inhabited.

Insects, which they variously classified as having the strains of beetles, gnats, wasps and bees, occasionally flitted amidst the trees, each insect as big as a normal starling wherever wings entered into it. Birds themselves appeared at times, sweeping across the purple heaven, some of them as large as eagles, with bat-like wings.

These things in themselves were fantastic enough, but they were not so strange as the unknowns that moved in the undergrowth and momentarily revealed themselves — travesties, freaks of the insect and animal kingdom, brought into being by the compound effect of radioactive soil and nutrition and the effects of cosmic radiation on the parents.

Then it became apparent that it was growing dark. The twilight seemed excessively brief, due to the gloom cast by the swaying vegetation. With the night, the stars glowed in a sky blacker than either Ken or Drew had ever seen. They contemplated it, watching for the telltale S of sparks which would show the downwardly moving path of the radio-guided projectile.

'These suits seem to be effectually

radiation-proof,' Ken commented at length through his audiophone. 'I don't feel any ill-effect from being out here, do you? And I suppose we're in the midst of cosmic rays at the moment?'

'Definitely we are,' Drew responded. 'Just the same, these suits are only makeshift. To wear them continuously would be intolerable, as we would have to do if we needed to be up here on the surface for any length of time. We — '

'There he is!' Ken interrupted abruptly, and pointed to a clear spot between the gargantuan treetops, where a trail of sparks was arcing swiftly down the sky and coming nearer.

Drew watched intently. If the radio guidance was correct, the projectile would land no more than a quarter of a mile from where he and Ken stood — and that was exactly what it did, its passage clearly marked by the forward jet's sparks, being operated by remote control, to act as a cushion to the projectile's descent.

Vegetation began to sizzle and explode in steam as the blasting heat of the exhaust struck it. Its immense weight carried the projectile downward without interception, branches and leaves smashing down before it. Then it hit the ground with a dull concussion. Immediately, Drew began hurrying towards the spot, with Ken beside him.

Outwardly, there was nothing wrong with the projectile: it was as undamaged as the moment when it had set off from the underworld. To unfasten the airlock by the emergency exterior clamp was only a moment's work, then Drew dragged a torch from his belt and flashed the bright beam into the dark, oblong interior. He fell back as a mighty hand struck at him violently. For a second or two he had a glimpse of an appalling gorilla-like face, with a flattened nose, receding forehead, and mighty fangs. The body of the creature, massive and hairy, had completely burst the clothing that now lay in a tangle on the floor.

Drew slammed the airlock and clamped it. The reflection from his torch cast on his grim, sweating features behind the face-visor.

'How in hell did *that* get in there?' Ken demanded. 'What became of Barry Johnson?'

'That *is* Barry Johnson, incredible though it seems. It has got to be! We know he left Earth and there was no gorilla present then. In fact, there isn't room for more than one body. It's Barry all right — atavised.'

'Cosmic radiation again?'

'What else?' Drew looked at the projectile again and sighed. 'I suppose we could open the airlock and shoot the poor devil, but he might get us first. In any case, he doesn't know he was Barry Johnson. Evidently space is too dangerous to cross at present. I'll have to break it to the folks as gently as I can.'

'And Bar — I mean the gorilla. What happens to him?'

'We'll have to let him die. No other way.'

'What about the automatic instrument readings on the origin of cosmic rays? Aren't you going to recover them?'

'We don't have to. Their findings are

being automatically transmitted back to our control room. I can study them when I get back.'

Drew turned back to the distant gap that led to the shaft and the underworld.

10

Upon returning to his headquarters, Drew studied the recorded information on cosmic radiation that the special instruments aboard the spaceship had discovered. Then he summoned the experts and controllers and explained the situation to them at the same time swearing them to secrecy.

'Nobody must know of this tragedy until I decide it is time,' he said quickly, studying the gloomy faces. 'It's enough to start a panic and that would be fatal down here.'

'Then what *are* we going to tell them?' an engineer demanded.

'I'll broadcast to them later. I won't tell them the space trip has proven a failure. I'll simply say 'operations are being carried out'.'

'In time they'll have to know,' Ken pointed out.

'They will, when I've prepared them.'

'This means space travel is ruled out?' somebody asked.

'I'm afraid so. Possibly there is a way to find a hundred per cent insulation against the cosmic rays, but it might be the work of a lifetime. In free space they evidently penetrate lead and interlocked atomic clusters.'

'What do you suppose caused Barry to slip back as he did?' Ken inquired.

'Throughout this ghastly business we have gained a new slant on the law of evolution,' Drew answered. 'It's upset a lot of preconceived theories. Evolution is a series of mutations from one stage to another, it having taken millions of years to raise us from the primordial ape — as Barry Johnson became — to the status of Man. It only took place at all because cosmic radiation has been so completely cut off from us by the magnetic field. In the beginning — the days of the gorillas, the Piltdown man, the monsters, and so forth — the cosmic rays were very prevalent: the magnetic field had not then built itself up to any great depth.

'As it became denser monsters ceased

191

to be born and man became semi-human, and then human. Until finally, as the magnetic field built up to maximum the harmful effect of cosmic radiation became negligible and Man became as we know him: As far as Barry was concerned, the full blast of cosmic rays ripped away the 'false front' that had made him a man, and he reverted to type.'

Drew paused, and studied his notes.

'So the mission was a complete failure?' Ken asked pointedly.

'Not entirely.' Drew looked up from his notes. 'The irony is that the flight *was* entirely successful in its primary mission — to trace the origin of the most destructive cosmic rays falling upon the Earth. The instruments aboard the craft showed that there is just one main source of the most destructive of them.'

'I find that hard to believe, Drew!' The objection came from one of the astronomical experts present. 'We've been studying them for more than forty years with space probes and telescopes, and it's been pretty well established that there is no single source. They are reaching us from all sections of the sky. They appear to come from supernova explosions — such as the Crab Nebula — and they are distributed all over the cosmos. More than 400 extragalactic supernovae have been recorded, and another two to three have been recorded in our own galaxy every hundred years, ever since astronomical records have been kept.'

Drew smiled faintly. 'An excellent summation, Andrews. But you are overlooking a vital factor. The Crab Nebula is over 2000 parsecs away from us, in the constellation of Taurus. Its emissions reaching us are greatly dissipated by the vast distance involved. But what if a neutron star was to explode much nearer to our solar system? At a distance of just — ' he picked up the top sheet of his notes — 'twenty light years?'

'My God,' Andrews said slowly. 'Are you telling us that you have discovered a recently exploded neutron star? One that is — astronomically speaking — almost on top of us?'

'I have,' Drew's voice was grim. 'It's emissions are travelling in a vast wave at almost the speed of light, and have just entered our solar system. Their intensity is almost undiminished, and may in fact have helped to trigger the trouble with our sun, combined with the coming together of the sunspot cycles that I had already predicted.'

A heavy quiet followed; then presently Ken got to his feet. 'All of which means exactly *what*?' he demanded.

'It means,' Drew answered quietly, 'that we are doomed. Ordinary cosmic rays are bad enough, but this new influx is many thousands of times more powerful than any previously known. Without its magnetic field, the Earth is a sitting duck.'

'But what about your space umbrella idea' Ken asked. 'Surely that can be tried, now that you know the exact location of the trouble?'

'You saw what happened to Barry Johnson, didn't you?' Drew snapped impatiently. 'There is no way we can send space engineers out into the deeps of space to erect any barrier. The best shielding we can manage on our space-ships proved to be totally inadequate.

Their crews would either die of radiation poisoning or atavise into apes long before they could even begin its assembly.'

Ken tightened his lips and looked round on the assembly. 'Well, now we know where we stand. All we can do now is get that city built and teach those who come after us to stand four-square to calamity.'

'As for me,' Drew said, 'I'll notify other Governments throughout the world what has happened. They must decide for themselves how best to let their respective peoples know the facts. As for our own people, I'll tell them tomorrow.'

And he did so, explaining that things were going 'according to plan.' Immediately afterwards boring continued on the last 1,000-feet of rock which would end the diagonal tunneling, and should cause them to meet the engineers of the neighbouring shaft. Once this happened the gouging out of the cavern for the city proper could commence. Drew now concentrated all his attention on making the underworld comfortable, realising that his battle to re-conquer space was, perhaps, a lost cause — for the time being, anyway.

At the change of shift one 'evening' he found Milly Morton awaiting him in his office. He frowned as he recognized her.

'Sorry to butt in,' she said in her insolent way.

Drew glanced at her dirty overalls and good-looking face.

'Have a seat, Miss Morton.'

'You remember me then?' She sat down near the desk.

'Naturally — and the plates! What do you want with me?'

'I'm wondering what happened to Barry Johnson.'

Drew settled in his swivel chair. 'You heard my broadcast, didn't you?'

'About 'everything going according to plan'? Oh, yes! But I don't care anything about plans. It's Barry in whom I'm interested.'

'Yes, he did mention he was volunteering for the space test because you had suggested it.'

'The idea, as I understood it, was for Barry to test space and then come back,'

Milly said. 'He told me that himself. That being so he ought to have returned some days ago. I've been wondering why he hasn't. All I want is an explanation.'

'Barry *did* come back, and has gone away again. He is no longer an ordinary citizen, but a selected man.'

Milly gave a disbelieving smile. 'You're not convincing me, Mr. Drew. If Barry were a protected person, a selected man, he'd still find a way to get to me.'

Drew waited, his face expressionless.

'I think,' Milly finished, a glint in her sapphire eyes, 'that the whole experiment failed, that Barry sailed on into space to his death, but you are soft-pedalling the information because of the repercussions it would produce after all the rosy things you've told the people.'

'I cannot stop you thinking,' Drew said.

'You won't stop me talking, either! Barry meant a lot to me, and for him to be just thrown away is more than I can stand. It amounts — to murder.'

'Hardly. Before he departed he signed a statement exonerating everybody from blame. He was a volunteer, and he did it only for you. Whether or not you are as loyal to him as he is to you is a matter of indifference to me.'

'I want visible proof that he is alive,' Milly snapped. 'If I don't get it I'll inform the people what has happened.'

Drew reflected for a moment or two, then he jerked his head.

'On your way, young woman! If you want to shout rumours from the house-tops, then shout them. I have enough faith in the people to believe that they won't credit you without proof — and that you haven't got.'

'Is that all you have to say?' Milly demanded.

'That's all. Get out!'

Milly got up, glared for a moment, then stalked from the office and slammed the door. Drew sat thinking.

'Wonder what the devil that girl's getting at?' he muttered. 'I'll swear she doesn't — or didn't — love Barry that much.'

And whilst he sat and tried to figure angles Milly returned to her billet where she showered and changed from workaday outfit into her best clothes. An hour after leaving Drew she arrived in all her glory in the office of Mortimer Bland.

She found him more or less cheerful. The fact that no more plates had collapsed had done much to raise a load from his mind.

'As delectable as ever, my dear,' he greeted her. 'You're a credit to the underworld.'

'I managed to wheedle the facts out of Drew,' Milly said, settling down and crossing her highly attractive legs. 'It was tough going, the way he feels about me, but I did it.'

'Good! What about space? Is it safe?'

'It's as safe as the Atlantic used to be before the Blight. Drew did not admit it openly, of course, but I gathered enough to know that Barry is at this very moment exploring for the source of cosmic rays — and using a machine sheathed as his, there is no danger at all in outer space.'

'Splendid!' Bland rubbed his fleshy hands together. 'That makes everything perfect. We can sail into the void, away from all this, and if necessary just go on cruising; or alternatively we can stay close to Earth and come back if things improve.'

Milly smiled. 'All you have to do now, Mort, is get the various engineers to tell you the exact specification of Barry's space projectile and have a machine made identical to it, only larger. From what I can gather, we shall have finished the present shaft boring in a week's time. When that happens the Northern and Midland shaft will converge, I suppose, and there will be a twelve-hour stoppage for celebration. Being amongst the workers I know all about that.'

'Which means what?'

'At that time, Drew, Ken West and all the other bigwigs will be so busy toasting each other it will be our moment to escape, providing the power engineer is bribed to open the shaft for the few moments when we need to depart. I'm assuming of course that our spaceship will be kept hidden in your own engineering works until the hour when it is needed.'

'I'll designate a special section to it,' Bland declared. 'Movable roof and everything. I shall have to learn how to activate the automatic pilot to control the machine, I suppose, but that shouldn't be difficult if the engineers and technicians concerned are paid enough . . . I have to hand it to you, Milly, you have definite organising talent even if you never were a good secretary.'

Milly laughed. 'I can organise as well as you can, Mort, when the end is something I specially desire.'

Bland laughed too, but somehow it had no conviction.

★ ★ ★

In the 'days' which followed, Milly reported for duty in the normal way, only seeing enough of Bland in her spare time to be assured that he had everything under control. Never by word or expression did she give any hint of the plot in her mind.

Drew, for his part, finding that no information was being handed out to the people by Milly, assumed that she had thought better of her threat and dismissed her from his mind. With Ken he supervised the final borings as with a supreme effort the last 800 — 500 — 300-feet were driven into the rocks, until, almost to the minute predetermined for the job, the ultimate mass of rock was destroyed and, as usual, transformed into dust by atomic blasters.

Through the dispersing haze in the glare of the huge arcs the workers stood staring into emptiness, but not for long. Beyond a distant ridge, floodlit, were moving figures armed with equipment.

A cry went up; then both communities surged forward with hands outflung in greeting to meet each other, and it was at this moment that Milly arrived in Bland's office, dressed in slacks and blouse in readiness for the anticipated journey. Bland was waiting for her, pacing up and down.

'Everything fixed?' Milly asked him quickly.

'Yes, my dear. I have the machine built and ready — priority job for my foundry

— and the powerhouse engineer is only waiting for my signal to open the shaft top. Everything else is taken care of. There are provisions, weapons, clothes, all we can need, in the flyer — together with books, writing materials, tapes and recordings, and needful etceteras for a protracted trip.'

'Then we'd better go,' Milly decided. 'We've a grand chance while the tomfoolery is going on.'

Bland nodded, nevertheless giving her a puzzled glance.

'Are you coming or not?' Milly demanded.

'Yes — of course. I was just wondering if I'd taken care of all details before departing.'

'What does it matter? By the time we come back — if we ever do — your present activities will be a memory.'

Bland strode forward, took the girl's arm, and led her by a private passage from the office into a one-time laboratory section now turned into a hangar in which stood the projectile. Milly paused for a moment and admired its tapering lines.

'Lovely! Positively lovely!' she declared.

'Everything to specification,' Bland said proudly.

Milly's eyes passed over the projectile again as it stood at its 45-degree angle.

'Placed exactly right for it to fly up the shaft,' Bland explained. 'I had the engineers do that for me, and I also know how to activate the robot pilot to control it. What pleases me is that once we are in free space we can coast along without any power. Something to do with constant velocity. Pretty good, eh? We only need power when pulling away from a big mass — like Earth — or approaching one, in which case the rockets are used to push us away. I've had a power plant put in with enough reserves to run continuously for five years non-stop. That ought to serve us.'

Milly did not seem disposed to ponder the technical details of the machine. Her appraisal of its exterior concluded, she ascended the ladder to the airlock and entered the gyroscopically-levelled control cabin. Here again everything seemed to be to her satisfaction. Bland came in behind her and shut the massive airlock.

'You realize,' he asked, switching on the roof light and looking at her steadily, 'just what we're going to do?'

'Only too well. Let's get started.'

Both of them lay down on the pneumatic couches and strapped themselves in.

Bland switched on the radio and gave orders over the private waveband to the powerhouse engineer. Two things happened a moment or so afterwards. First the roof of the hangar, electrically controlled from the powerhouse not far distant, rolled back, and beyond it there became visible the towering blackness of the shaft. Bland gazed at it for a moment through the bowed observation window, Milly peering across over his shoulder.

'Okay, Mr. Bland,' came a voice over the radio. 'The shaft cover is open. The rest is up to you. We'll close the shaft when you've gone.'

Bland switched off the radio and activated the robot pilot.

'This is it, my dear,' he murmured, as power began to hum in the plant in the ship's tail. 'Watch that power lever.'

She followed his gaze, watched fascinated as the lever, obeying the invisible electrical impulses of the auto-pilot, moved to its first notch.

Silent, both of them fascinated by the speed and apparent lightness of the machine, Bland and Milly watched the shaft walls hurtling past them. They saw the shaft opening appear. It was clouded over with the fury of a storm and no stars were visible.

The machine cleared the shaft opening cleanly and hurtled in vertical ascent into the midst of whirling bolts of lightning. A storm of cataclysmic violence was raging, in the midst of which nothing could be seen except caverns of nimbus cloud and the interplay of forked lightning.

It was terrifying in its nearness and brilliance, but even so it could not penetrate the neutralizing walls of the machine. As they became gradually aware that they were safe Bland and Milly relaxed a little, narrowing their eyes against the lightning and watching anxiously for the moment when they could burst free of the storm level.

The needle of the altimeter crept higher and higher as the power plant hummed steadily. Kept on even keel by the gyroscopes controlling the cabin, the two within had no sensation of the machine itself being vertical beyond the fact that they could feel their backs pressing into their pneumatic couches.

Then, so abruptly it was startling, the machine flashed through the last layer of storm cloud and sailed onwards and upwards into a violet sky blazing with stars. The sun was there, masked and wan, the great cancer of the sunspots still eating out most of its formerly brilliant photosphere. Milly looked at it intently and gave a grim smile.

'*That* sun will never recover, Mort, even if we wait until Doomsday,' she said. 'I don't know much about astronomy, but I *do* know when anything is dying. And that sun certainly is! Hardly as bright as a full moon.'

Bland nodded. He was too absorbed in the majesty of space with its myriad twinkling stars and the distant whirling mass of the Andromeda Nebula to pass any comment. And clear though the view was it became even clearer as the last traces of the stratosphere were left behind and the machine still hurtled on at a steady velocity, climbing now in free space. Below, the Earth — relying on solar light for reflection — was hardly visible against the abysmal dark of infinity.

'Well, so far so good,' Bland commented at length. 'That winking light is telling us we can unstrap and leave our couches. From what the engineers told me the robot pilot won't start relaxing the accelerative power until we have got to about three thousand miles — that faint crescent over there is the moon, I take it? Hardly visible because of lack of sunlight. The auto-pilot will be altering our course shortly to lose the pull of the lunar attraction which will leave us the empty void ahead.'

'Just as we want it,' Milly said. 'I'll fix up a meal for us meanwhile.'

Bland grinned. 'We'd better make the most of it. It could be our last proper meal for some time. When the acceleration shuts down we'll be in freefall, and will have to make do with concentrates and bulbs with straws!'

Milly turned away and began an exploration of the vessel until she found the storage rooms and some tinned and bottled necessities. She ignored the zero-gravity provisions. Since the speed of acceleration was just sufficient to keep a gravitational pull almost equivalent to Earth-norm she had no difficulty in moving around. At length she had laid a spread that made Bland gaze in surprise.

'Good as a banquet!' he exclaimed, grinning. 'What's it for? To celebrate?'

Milly glanced at him. 'The condemned prisoners usually have a good meal to finish up with, don't they?'

'Eh?' Bland's grin faded a little; then it came back. 'Sure they do, but you could use a less disquieting simile.'

With the automatic pilot flying the ship perfectly, he came over to the console Milly was using as an improvised table and seated himself on one of the stools affixed to the metal floor.

Milly sat down too and poured out wine very deliberately. Bland took one of the glasses she handed to him.

'When I said the condemned prisoners usually have a good meal with which to finish up, I wasn't joking,' she said, and her blue eyes pinned him.

'What the devil *are* you talking about?' he asked irritably. 'We got away, didn't we? Just as we'd planned? Here we are, alone, uninterrupted, and — '

'Doomed!' Milly finished for him. 'We're committing suicide, Mort, you and I. I am doing so willingly. You, I think, will not be quite so satisfied about it.'

Bland looked uncomprehending. Milly gave him a cynical smile and then continued: 'You didn't really think I had forgotten the way you threw me out in New Delhi, did you? You don't suppose I was elated when I had to live as best I could, getting in and out of all kinds of dives, scraping a living here, there, and everywhere, all because you didn't stand by me when I temporarily lost my looks and youth. I didn't forget one bit of it — and I've worked for a long time

210

for this moment.'

Drew put down his wine glass so forcibly it splintered at the stem. He watched the red liquid flow swiftly from the glass cup as it rocked back and forth beside his hand.

'Come out into the open and talk straight!' he commanded.

'What's your hurry?' Milly asked languidly. 'We've all the time there is . . . My plan began from the moment when I heard the rumour that Drew wanted to see if it was possible to travel in space safely again. It dawned on me that, in space, if death struck you down, nobody would be able to see it coming and perhaps give you medical aid to bring you back to life — as would probably have happened on Earth if I'd shot you, or something like that. I wanted to have you alone and watch you die beside me — unwillingly, yet compelled to do so. That, to my mind, would be exquisite revenge.'

Bland sat listening, oblivious to the wine that dripped over the table edge on to his costly trousers.

'Before I could make sure that space is a deathtrap I had to find a way of testing it — so I used Barry Johnson. The poor fool wanted to be heroic, he said, and at my suggestion volunteered for a space journey test. It was possible, of course, that space might be safe. If so, I was prepared to think of something else. However, events turned out otherwise and Barry Johnson either died in space or else he was lost. He certainly did not return to Earth else he would have sought me out.'

'You said he had discovered space was safe!' Bland snapped.

'I know I did — to get you out here, where you are now. When I saw Drew he hedged sufficiently to satisfy me that Barry Johnson had met with disaster. I told you the exact opposite — and so here we are in the void, heading I assume for whatever fate it was that overtook Barry.'

'You're crazy, Milly,' Bland said. 'Even if Drew did not admit openly that Barry had succeeded, he didn't admit that he had *failed*. You jumped to conclusions.'

'No.' Milly shook her blonde head. 'I

knew from what Drew said — and the fact that beyond one broadcast he never referred to the matter again — that Barry went to his death.'

'Which is more than we are doing,' Bland retorted. 'We are okay, are we not? And the moment we've had this meal we're going straight back to Earth. What is more we'll turn this to account and tell Drew that, whatever may have happened to Barry, we have proved that space can be crossed safely. Turn everything to advantage — that's the way to get on!'

'Before I go back to Earth I'll kill you, Mort,' Milly stated deliberately; and Bland found himself looking at the automatic she had drawn stealthily from the pocket of her slacks. 'I came out here because I want to die! And you shall die with me. There was no future in that underground hell hole. I couldn't stand another minute of being buried alive — growing older, working harder, ruled by that inhuman devil Anton Drew and his scientific decisions. I heard enough to know that Drew does not expect life to return to Earth's surface for at least a century. Death is preferable to that. Death is also preferable to travelling endlessly through space with a swine like you!'

'When I said you're mad, I was right,' Bland muttered.

'The hell hole was enough to make anybody mad, wasn't it? Not you, I suppose, with your money and influence; but to anybody like me, kicked around, with no friends and no future — Yes, maybe I am mad,' Milly admitted. 'Even if I am, I am not afraid to die — and I look forward to seeing you die, too.'

'How?' Bland asked. 'You can shoot me, I suppose — but you could have done that back on Earth. Just what do you think is going to happen to us in space here? Look at us! As fit as the moment we left Earth.'

'So far,' Milly assented. 'But something happened to Barry Johnson, and since this machine is a duplicate of his it should also happen to us. He was a trained pilot, able to stand this kind of thing better than we can — yet he never came back. Why? Did he die, burn up, go crazy, leap

214

into space, or what? Whatever it was, we'll do it too.'

Bland was silent, convinced Milly was a lunatic, yet with a lunatic's gift for clever scheming. Presently he got to his feet. Going to the storage cupboard he took out a fresh wineglass and — followed constantly by Milly's automatic — returned to the table and poured out some wine for himself. He drank it slowly and then smiled.

'How do you suppose I reached eminence, Milly?' he asked presently; and the girl looked surprised,

'By stamping on everybody's face, I suppose. I can't see it matters when I have the last word.'

'Don't be too sure that you have . . . I reached eminence by thinking faster than the next man — or woman. My suspicions were instantly aroused when you suggested going into space would be more comfortable than remaining on Earth. I don't know much about science, but I do know — as does any informed adult in this space age — that there is no gravity in deep space. As I remarked a few minutes back, as soon as our present acceleration ceases, we'll be in freefall and will just float about. Normal activities will be impossible, as will be consuming food and drink normally. and — ' he grinned coarsely — 'excreting it! A protracted spaceflight — especially to untrained people like ourselves — will be close to absolute hell!'

'I know nothing about that!' Milly snapped. 'Science bunk never interested me — '

'You're lying. Years ago, perhaps so. But once you took up your relationship with Barry Johnson — him training to be an astronaut — he would have been bound to tell you all about it, in order to impress you. Telling you what privations he would face in order to win your affection!' Bland smiled as he saw Milly's expression change.

'I'm right, aren't I?'

Milly remained silent, tight-lipped.

'I quickly realised,' Bland resumed, 'that you never had the slightest intention of remaining in space for any length of time. I admit I had not the vaguest idea what you were planning — this suicide plan of yours — but I did think it prudent to check up on space travel before I plunged into it. So I questioned the chief engineer who supervised the construction of Barry's projectile. I can tell you what did happen to Barry.'

'What?' Milly's voice was a dry whisper.

'He became an ape, because of the action of cosmic rays. The engineer was present when Drew gave an explanation on what had happened, and it was decided to hush things up. I didn't see risking going into space with that possibility hanging over me, yet I wanted to find out what your little game was and why you'd handed me such a story.'

Milly sat waiting, her automatic resting on the table edge.

'The engineer told me that the probable reason for Barry's death was that he was unprotected by a wall of insulation between himself and the outer shell of the machine, which made it possible for the cosmic rays to strike through at him even through lead and specially made window glass. He showed me a plan he had worked out for himself, and which he intended giving to Drew in order that a new attempt could be made. The particular machine he had in mind was identical to Johnson's — except for size — but the control cabin was an independent unit balanced on gyroscopes so it could remain level. In a word, a ship within a ship . . .

'The machine we are now in is an example of it,' Bland continued. 'Between the walls of this control room and the outer sheathed wall of the machine itself is two feet of emptiness. Or at least it would seem empty to the naked eye. Actually, powerful magnetic streams are being forced through it, all fed by atomic power from the plant. They have the effect of dragging aside the showers of cosmic radiation that pierce the insulated outer hull and discharge them through electrical chambers in the machine's tail. That's as near as I can explain it to you, being an unscientific man. It's as though showers of needles are being fired at us, but never reach us because the magnetic stream drags them aside. So we in here are completely unaffected by cosmic rays. We are inside a flawlessly insulated shell. As long as the plant operates we are safe.'

Milly's eyes strayed to it and Bland grinned.

'It is housed in an unbreakable casing,' he said. 'There is nothing you can do to smash it up. The heart of anything must always be well protected. So, Milly, that engineer has the right idea. I paid him a million pounds there and then to transfer the copyright of his plan to me and say nothing to Drew; because, don't you see, with it a proven success I can get another fortune from those who wish to use Bland space machines in which to travel into space and perhaps erect some barrier to save the Earth. I made this trip into space — at the same time apparently falling in with your views — at the risk of my life to see if I really had got something. Now I know I have.'

'You've forgotten the window,' Milly said. 'If cosmic radiation doesn't come through that I'll be surprised!'

Bland chuckled. 'It isn't a window, m'dear. It is a clear glass frame with a reflector beyond it. How otherwise could you see from a shell inside a shell, both of them never being in the same identical position for more than a few seconds at a time? On the outer hull is a transmitter, similar to a television pick-up eye, which transmits to the reflector the scene outside. It gives the impression of looking through a window on to the void, with the one difference that no cosmic radiation can penetrate. Even the inner and outer airlocks are not in line unless the master-switch over there is closed. That levels the gyroscope and brings inner and outer shells into alignment.'

Silence. Bland relaxed, toying with his glass of wine.

'Apparently, m'dear, your fancy work didn't get you very far,' he commented. 'I've found out what sort of a girl you really are and conquered the dangers of space at the same time. When I return to Earth with my information, as I intend, my discovery will net me a fortune and earn Drew's blessing. That will cancel out my other — er — mistake in making faulty plates.'

'I won't stand for it!' Milly shouted abruptly, jumping to her feet and levelling the automatic. 'I'll see you — '

She got no further. Suddenly the contents of Bland's wineglass dashed into her face, and in the split second of shock he had snatched the gun from her and put it in his pocket.

'Better think again, Milly,' he suggested, handing her a handkerchief. 'Nobody can make rings round Mortimer Bland.'

Milly dried her face. Resignation came slowly to her features.

'All right,' she said, shrugging. 'You win. What do you propose to do with me when we return to Earth?'

'Turn you loose to go wherever you will, safe in the knowledge that there is nothing you can ever do to me. I don't hate you enough to want to murder you so you can go your way and I'll go mine. And that will be that.'

'Perhaps,' Milly responded ambiguously — then with a movement so swift Bland had no time to grasp her intentions she hurtled across the control room and

221

slammed home the master-switch controlling the airlocks.

Bland dived. Milly swung, slamming up her bunched knuckles into Bland's face so that his teeth jarred. In that split second she wrenched down the single lever controlling the clamps of both inner and outer airlocks.

The locks opened inwards so that air pressure inside the machine would not force the locks open against the non-pressure of the vacuum outside — which was a factor with which Milly had not reckoned. To tug them open was as impossible as trying to raise herself by her own shoelaces. She dragged impotently at the inner door, its clamps off, but on that door there was a uniform pressure of fourteen pounds to the square inch. Only when atmosphere of similar density existed outside could the door be budged.

Then Bland had seized her and flung her savagely across the control room. She hit the wall and collapsed, her blonde hair streaming over her face. Bland slammed the lever back in place and pulled the master-switch out of engagement.

'Not much good, Milly, is it?' he asked, his eyes glinting. 'And we're going back to Earth this moment!'

Milly remained where she was, hardly moving, her fallen hair hiding her expression. She was cudgeling her unscientific brain to remember something she had once read as a schoolgirl — a scientific adventure story it had been, about some girls on a trip to Mars. Acceleration had pinned them down because it was too rapid, and then they had . . .

Milly gave a grim smile to herself. Bland was over sixty, and strong though his heart might be she doubted if it could stand violent strain continuously applied. Gradually she got to her feet and lurched to the control board looking down on Bland as he sat before the switches. He was busily studying the panel and a notebook, where the Chief Engineer had written down the operation of the robot controls. He did not notice Milly's gaze straying to the main power lever, which he had identified to her earlier.

It was only in its second notch,

maintaining steady velocity against Earth's gravity-field. There were five other notches, which should only be built up in stages if the full power of the atomic plant were to be used.

Milly acted.

In one sweeping movement her hand came down and slammed the power lever to the furthest notch. Instantly the full flood of discharging energy in the atom plant transferred itself into the rear rocket tubes. The machine darted forward from seemingly leisurely speed towards ultimate velocity in the space of as many seconds as it took to overcome inertia.

The effect was overwhelming, even for Milly, who had been half expecting it. She crashed on the floor instantly and lay on her face, unable to move hand or foot, nailed down by the frightful speed of the machine as it streaked with staggering velocity through the gulf.

Bland, unable to get up from the control chair, felt it twang and creak under his weight — a weight of immeasurable tons, it seemed. He had the ghastly feeling of sinking into himself.

Organ was crushed into organ as the speed still mounted. He was telescoped until his heart refused to function and his breath died in deflated lungs. Dead, he sat with hands on the switches, their handles embedded a quarter of an inch into his palms.

Milly, lighter in weight, and younger, took longer to die — but every moment was exquisite anguish. Unable to raise her head she did not see Bland's last moments, the very thing she had always wanted. All she could see was the metal floor on which she was pinned. Then it seemed as steel plates were bearing down on her spine, that her breasts and thighs were being squashed relentlessly into metal. Lights flashed and gyrated through the raging torment in her skull — then she could no longer draw breath. Her heart stopped and smothered her in obliterating dark.

The projectile flew on, its velocity still mounting, its plant capable of carrying it on at increasing speed for quite three more weeks — after which, unless deflected by some body or other, it would retain that velocity. And with it went the man who had bought the secret of safely crossing space, and the girl who had wanted to see him die and had been cheated after all.

11

Operations were well under way for the gouging of the giant main cavern before the disappearance of Mortimer Bland was noticed. After an interval of several chronometer days had elapsed, Drew having no reason to contact the tycoon, it became apparent that he was nowhere in the underworld . . . Then it was found that Milly Morton had not reported for work and that she, too, was absent.

'But where do you suppose Bland's gone?' Ken asked in surprise, when Drew talked the matter over with him. 'If he and the Morton girl were anywhere down here they'd have been found by now.'

'Only one answer, Ken: they've gone into space.'

'Then heaven help them! By this time they'll be apes'

'I wonder,' Drew mused. 'Bland was not the kind of man to make any big move without weighing everything up. If he and the Morton girl did go into space I'm willing to bet that Bland knew all about the possibilities ahead of him before he started. Doesn't that suggest that somehow he may have discovered how to cross space in *safety*?'

'Perhaps,' Ken admitted. 'But I don't see how a man as unscientific as Bland could ever think up anything like that. Anyway, he'd be back by now if he'd made a successful trip, wouldn't he?'

'I'm going to look into this,' Drew decided — and so, for some days afterwards whenever he could spare time, he conducted an investigation on his own account. By degrees he got most of the details of Bland's secret spaceship construction, of the bribing of the powerhouse engineer to open the shaft, and finally the hint that the chief engineer who had built the Johnson projectile had also designed Bland's — to a different specification. Accordingly the engineer found himself summoned to a full meeting of the scientists who controlled the underworld, Drew as usual, acting as chairman.

'Mr. Standish,' he said quietly, 'you are not here on trial or anything like that, but to answer questions. We have it on record that you oversaw construction of a spaceship privately for Mr. Bland, the materials being from Bland's own reserves.'

'Correct, sir,' Standish admitted quietly.

'You are aware that that constituted a breach of law, in so far that no engineering project is permitted without the sanction of this assembly?'

'I suppose I was in the wrong, but — '

'You *were*!' Drew snapped. 'However, an issue arises. It appears Mr. Bland's machine was different from Johnson's. What is the explanation?'

'It was larger. Mr. Bland wanted a control room big enough for two people, and also other chambers for sleeping and — '

'Never mind the amenities, Mr. Standish. You must have the original plan from which you worked. Where is it?'

'I destroyed it, sir. Mr. Bland had a duplicate, but I don't know what he did with it.'

Drew's face became grim. 'Recently you placed a draft in your bank for a million pounds, signed by Mortimer Bland. A sum so huge could not be for services rendered. It was for something of exceptional value — and Bland wouldn't pay that kind of money without being sure of a handsome profit. In your capacity you could have nothing of extreme value to offer — unless perhaps it was an original idea or invention.'

The engineer hesitated and then nodded. 'That was the reason, sir — and there the matter ended as far as I am concerned. I can't be expected to reveal what the original idea was since I sold it to Mr. Bland.'

'Technically, perhaps not,' Drew agreed, 'but where you're in the wrong is in selling to an individual any idea of importance before consulting us — the Assembly. That makes your deal with Bland void because you had no official sanction. You should have placed your idea before us, and had it been worthwhile you would have been paid a fair price for it. If not, you would then have been at liberty to dispose of it as you wished. As things are, Mr. Standish, orders have been given for the cancellation of Bland's draft to you. The deal is off! I'm sorry, but you know how tough our regulations are if we're to keep order down here.'

'Which means,' Standish said slowly, 'that I get nothing at all for my idea? Bland has it and has paid for it. He'll go on using it and have the money as well. That's unfair!'

'The answer is that you hand the idea to us. If we like it we'll pay for it at Government rate. When Bland returns to our midst — if he does — he will be informed that he has no monopoly over your idea and his money will be refunded. In fact that will happen anyway when the bank makes his draft illegal.'

Nobody said anything for a moment or two. In fact most of the assembly was admiring the way Drew had wangled things round to his own advantage whilst still staying within the framework of underworld law. Then Standish made up his mind.

'My idea, gentlemen, was to — '

He paused, startled, and the others looked about them as a growling rumble, becoming ever louder, began to beat upon their ears, setting the headquarters trembling.

'Shaft collapse!' Ken cried, leaping up. 'Get out — '

He dived for the door but was not quick enough. With shattering violence rock and metal plates from high up the shaft came raining down on the headquarters' temporary building, perched as it was on the edge of the Fifth Level.

Ken went down into darkness with the weight of countless tons pressing upon him. Drew half reached the doorway and was then flung senseless against the wall. The lights went out and the headquarters crumbled and smashed as the avalanche thundered past the Fifth Level and rained into the lower depths. Here it did little damage since most of the workers were busy in the cavern and out of the shaft.

There was a momentary stunning silence in the depths; then with the activity of ants everybody sprang to life, and for the second time in the fantastic history of the underworld rescue work began, this time on a bigger scale than hitherto.

Of these activities neither Drew nor Ken had any knowledge. When they recovered they were in beds, side by side, in a mobile hospital, surgeons anxiously watching them. By stages both men discovered how much of them was left.

Ken had a half-healed scar down one side of his face, which would be there for the rest of his life, and both legs had been broken. Drew had escaped all minor troubles but had one major one in the loss of his left arm. He stoically absorbed the information. Eventually he would be given an artificial one.

'What else happened?' was his main inquiry.

A shaft foreman was ready with the answers.

'The headquarters was wiped out, sir. We've fixed up new ones on the lowest level, where the cavern is being cut.'

'And the Assembly? How many survived?'

'Just — you and Mr. West, sir.'

Drew tightened his lips. 'All those valuable scientists wiped out! Chief-engineer Standish as well, I suppose?'

'Yes, sir.'

Ken, who had been listening in silence, gave Drew a hopeless glance. Drew reflected for a moment.

'And the cause of the collapse? Have you traced it?'

'Faulty plates, sir, high up. We've repaired the damage. More collapses may occur in time: just have to risk it. And, unfortunately, with Mr. Bland not being here, we can't question him. He hasn't come back. Perhaps he knew what would happen.'

'Perhaps,' Drew agreed. 'All right, thanks; you've done your best. The new Assembly, apparently, will consist of Mr. West and myself. Keep working on the cavern.'

'We are doing, sir. Another month should finish it.'

The foreman departed and, left to themselves, Ken and Drew exchanged looks.

234

'Which would seem to be that,' Drew commented, studying the flattened sleeve of his pyjama jacket. 'We'll never know now what it was that Standish sold to Bland — unless Bland comes back, which I think extremely unlikely.'

'I wonder,' Ken mused, 'what the chances are of finding notes about Standish's plan in his billet? I know he said he destroyed the plan when he sold it to Bland, but there may still be references to it, which would help us. Or maybe we can find the copy of the plan in what is left of Bland's workshops or personal quarters.'

'Possible. The moment we're discharged we'll look.'

And they did. Their official positions gave them the right to probe and examine where they chose, but they drew blank just the same. There was no sign of anything in Standish's billet, or in his bank.

Nor was there anything to be found in Bland's headquarters. Presumably he had the copy of the plan with him.

'That seems to be the end of it,' Drew

said, when everything, had been tried. 'Maybe we missed something valuable; maybe we didn't.'

'What about questioning some of the construction workers who worked under Standish?' Ken suggested.

Drew shrugged. 'Since Bland has never returned, it suggests that Standish's invention wasn't viable after all. No, let's forget it. We've other things to do.'

And, characteristically, he thereafter threw his whole tremendous energy into the task of supervising, with Ken, the creation of the cavern where the city was to stand.

* * *

With the non-return of Mortimer Bland and no more shaft collapses the memory of him faded from those who worked on and began to see the city take form. By now, prepared by one or two speeches from Drew, most of the people realised subconsciously that the attempt to master space and perhaps neutralise cosmic radiation had failed.

There was no savage reaction to the disappointment. One or two workers became threatening but had to fall in line with those who were still loyal to Drew.

Then, after six months of furious activity, in which time the British city had grown to almost complete size, Drew found himself facing a totally different problem. He had known it must arise some day, but when it did he felt somehow unprepared to do battle with it. It involved so much that was heartbreaking in the matter of decisions.

There arrived, first in twos and threes, then in growing numbers, the forerunners of the freaks. Very few parents registered the births of their children — though it was compulsory — for fear inquiry would reveal what queer children they were and order their elimination. But nobody could avoid noticing the weird new offspring as time passed. Both girls and boys were affected, it seemed, and the freakishness begotten of cosmic radiation made every one different in some peculiarity.

Some were long-legged and tiny-bodied; others had huge heads and little round bodies with hardly any legs at all. In others, the hands touched the ground. In certain cases the freakishness took the form of dazzling beauty of features, particularly in the females: otherwise it was expressed in bulging eyes, button-mouths, and atrophied shoulders.

To Drew, who had perforce collected reports of the new generation for study, it was like watching a series of scenes in a distorting mirror as he and the surgical experts he had gathered around him — Ken being there as a matter of course — saw the movie films which had been made over a period of months.

'Insanity!' Drew whispered, when the reel had unwound itself. 'Some two hundred children and only two amongst them look normal — and even they are not. I mean those two girls, so beautiful they're breathtaking. The rest are hideous, and it will become worse unless we act. Imagine some of those appalling girls and boys marrying when they are adult. Their children would be more hideous still!'

'They must be eliminated,' said the head surgeon.

'You mean euthanasia?' Drew glanced at him. 'Simple to say, but hard to put into practice when it means killing off two hundred children who are happy enough, even if they are freaks. They enjoy life down here because they have never known any other.'

'We are concerned only with the purity of the race,' the surgeon answered phlegmatically. 'If we are not to breed monsters those children must be eliminated. Only two of them can be spared — the two girls with the beautiful faces. We shall have to wait until two boys of similarly normal characteristics arrive before we can think of producing a mating strain.'

Drew was silent, his brows knitted.

'Nothing else for it, Anton,' Ken said. 'You can't let your heart rule your head over this issue.'

'Certainly not!' the surgeon snapped. 'Just give me the word, Mr. Drew, and I'll do the rest.'

'All right, go ahead,' Drew said, shrugging. 'And if the parents of the children lead a revolution to depose me I shan't be surprised!'

The surgeon departed before Drew could change his mind. Then Ken asked a question:

'Has it occurred to you, Anton, that if we go on having freaks born, as we probably shall, the race will die out? It will end when we older ones die. I know we have those two girls who seem to be all right, but if they grow up and no normal males are born to mate with them, what then?'

'I can't answer that now, Ken. We'll see what we get in the births that are still to come. Meantime, I had better prepare myself for the wrath of the parents concerned.'

And Drew had not miscalculated, either. Some hundreds of men and women, loving their children, queer though they might be, vented their fury on Drew and all his methods when it was discovered that euthanasia had been used in every case except that of the two beautiful little girls.

To explain to the infuriated mothers and fathers that it was necessary to kill to preserve the purity of the race was a waste of time. Drew was called a murderer, and the head surgeon a baby-killer. Fearing for the fate of the two girls who had been spared Drew had them taken into protective custody until the fury of the deprived ones had died down.

Then it was that the surgeon made a discovery. The two girls certainly had beauty in excelsis, but even on them the cosmic radiation had been at work before their birth. It had not been apparent in the film what the defect was, but the surgeon discovered it immediately. Neither child could see or hear. The necessary nerves were absent — so the beautiful children followed the others into the drowsy sleep of death.

The move did much to save Drew. It looked as though there was no favouritism, and gradually his position became as secure as before. Slowly, as the city grew to its full power and was divided up into communities — as months passed and throughout the world other cities developed, it was brought home to those of childbearing age that it was probably no use having children anyway. If they turned out abnormal that would be the finish of them. So, all over the world, the birthrate began to nose-dive, further slashed by the fact that every time a freak appeared it was eliminated.

'Where are we heading, Anton?' Ken asked, one 'morning', looking from the window of Drew's office onto the vast spread of the internal city. 'We've built the city and domiciled ourselves. We keep in touch with the ways of other cities by radio and TV. We have everything; yet, we have nothing. We're a dying race. How much longer do you think children will continue to be freaks? Surely, down here, we are protected from cosmic radiation?'

'No doubt of it. The Geiger counters prove it.'

'Then why do we keep having freaks when the parents are as normal as you or I?'

Drew gave a tired smile. 'The answer lies in the fact that every man and woman who at present is able to have children was formerly on the surface, and affected by radiation. Apparently it has produced a permanently warping effect that remains in the parental germ plasm as long as the owner lives. The only hope would be one normal child of each sex, from whom, as they reached adult life, others could stem. But a vicious circle seems to preclude that possibility.'

'That leaves us two choices,' Ken said. 'Either we adults perish when our time runs out, and the end will be an empty world and the finish of the human race — or we try and find synthetic life. Create! If only we could do that. One man and one woman. The rest would take care of itself.'

'Can't be done.' Drew shook his head. 'I've had it over with the head surgeon. To create the outline of a man or woman and give him or her every necessary organ and attribute is not too difficult — but can we fan *life* into the dead clay? No! Every known combination of radiation and chemical reaction has been tried, without result. In the years gone by man had

243

talked glibly of synthesis of life. But when you really get down to it, it can't be done.'

Ken nodded moodily; then Drew said slowly: 'There is one other possibility, however. That is — adaptability. It is said that the human animal is the most adaptable creature ever created. Our living down here when we are really surface creatures is one proof of it. Suppose, though, we could develop a race of men and women who could live on the surface, adapted to its cosmic radiations, its darkness, and its cold? Like produces like. In time, the offspring would be like the parents. In adapting them to the new conditions surgical science would be used to make even the mechanisms of parenthood adaptable to cosmic radiation — which would not mean freaks but a reproduction of the parent, as in normal birth. It is a vast, involved technique, but if we could do it we'd have a new race with a totally different outward appearance to ourselves.'

'And whom do you suppose would be willing to undertake an experiment like that? Few have forgotten how completely Barry Johnson threw himself away.'

'True, but there are always bold spirits of both sexes who would volunteer, especially those weary of conditions down here and willing to try something fresh.' There was a gleam in Drew's eyes. 'It's a gamble, Ken, but worth it.'

And upon that note Drew departed to consult the head surgeon and biological experts.

'Yes, there's no reason why we shouldn't try it,' the head surgeon agreed. 'In the past, science has trained men and women to stand the rigours of the Arctic and the heat of the Tropics. It has also made them able to travel faster than sound and endure the stratosphere, and — before the recent influx of cosmic rays — even space, without harm. I see no reason why we shouldn't produce people who, through glandular and other changes, should not withstand out-surface conditions.'

'You'll need exact reports on surface conditions?' Drew asked.

'Definitely. Day by day reports.'

'I'll see to it,' Drew promised, 'and I'll also call for volunteers for the experiment.'

With that he left and, wasting no time, gave a broadcast to the city's inhabitants, explaining the circumstances and asking for men and women who cared to step forward. To his surprise, a dozen men and women arrived in the office not half an hour after his broadcast. Each of them was young and having all the enthusiasm of their age.

'Very gratifying,' Drew commented, smiling, his one hand resting on the desk. 'Twelve of each sex. What prompted this?'

'We represent the League of the Future, sir,' one of the young men explained.

'The what?'

'Just a designation. We've banded ourselves together in a sort of club, our aim being to do whatever we can to lighten the load of the older folks down here who find it tough going. We are pretty sure that a day will come, thanks to none of us being over twenty-five, when we'll go back to the surface and live as we did before the Blight. For the older ones that may never happen — so what more natural than we should try and cheer them up a bit?'

'You're all to be congratulated!' Drew declared warmly. 'However, you realise what your volunteering may mean?'

'All of us do, and all of us have decided to risk it. Only the young and more or less physically perfect can undertake an experiment of this kind. If we don't who can? We're as willing to experiment as if there was an invader in our midst.'

'The old spirit still burns!' Drew exclaimed, rising. 'And whilst it does, this human race of ours can never die. All you have to do is report to the head surgeon and leave the rest to him. The experiment is his province, not mine.'

Moving to the office door, he opened it for the party and watched them file out into the long corridor. As he saw them go he felt that his faith in human nature was restored — then the sound of the visiphone buzzer broke his chain of thought. Crossing to the desk he switched on the instrument.

'Yes? Drew here.'

'Latest surface reports, sir. Solar bolometer reading is eighteen hundred; sunspot area stationary; maximum day temperature touches — '

'Wait!' Drew interrupted sharply. 'Did you say the sunspot area had become *stationary*?'

'Yes, sir.' The face of the astronomical worker perched high up in the shaft where stood No. I Dome, looked into the tele-plate. 'For the last few weeks the Earth has been bombarded by massive solar flares, but they eventually ceased last week. Since when, there has been no flares and no extension of spots for the last four days.'

'Good!' Drew breathed, his eyes gleaming. 'Very good! Let me see those plates — '

The technician held them up so that the telescreen reproduced them in short focus for Drew's critical eyes. He compared them, the sunspot areas marked out by mathematical squares. There was no doubt about it: both plates were identical, showing no increase in sunspot extension.

'Many thanks,' he said at length. 'Relay

the information to the surgical laboratory.' He switched off and then contacted central headquarters where Ken was in charge of operations. Ken's face appeared almost immediately on the screen.

'Hello, Anton!' he greeted. 'Something the matter? You look quite excited — for you!'

'I've reason to be,' Drew responded. 'I just got news that the sunspots have stopped spreading! Over four days and no increase! You realise what that means?'

Ken gave a start. 'I should think I do . . . The sun might go back to normal! That's it, isn't it?'

'Not quite as good as that, but it does mean that if they don't get any larger the sun will not collapse into a white dwarf after all — and, in time, as the cycle declines, will regain its normal power and brilliance. Slowly, the magnetic field will build up again, until finally — until finally,' Drew finished, 'the surface will be as it was before the Blight came.'

Ken gave a dry laugh. 'Which means all this fuss and palaver has been for nothing — or almost. In a few years — '

'No, Ken. Normalcy will not return in our lifetime. I'm still convinced it will take nearly a century for this solar disaster to right itself. Even after that happens many more years must pass before the radioactive soil breaks down into normal compounds. We at least have finished with the surface, but for those who are made adaptable to the present surface conditions, if it can be done, it means conditions will get slowly better, which will give them and their offspring the chance to accustom themselves. Evolution will have to begin all over again. Twelve men and twelve women will form the nucleus of the new race.'

'Twelve! You think you'll get that many?'

'I have got them. They're in the laboratory now.'

12

Six weeks after the experiment in adaptability had commenced, the head surgeon arrived in Drew's office one 'morning', looking as impartial and gauntly inhuman as ever.

'Good to see you again, doctor,' Drew greeted him.

'Thank you.' The surgeon seated himself as Drew motioned; then he added quietly: 'I'm afraid we must write off adaptability.'

A chill descended on Drew. 'But — why?'

'Because you can go just so far in tampering with Nature, and no farther. I half-expected it, but didn't commit myself until I was sure. As it is, the only result of the experiment is a dead man and a dead woman. The remainder of the volunteers are untouched and may as well return to the normal, so-called, life. I'm here to report the deaths. I have signed statements exonerating myself and the staff from blame.'

'But what the devil happened?' Drew demanded blankly.

'Everything!' The surgeon shook his head moodily. 'In the first place, the main necessity is to so alter the nervous system that it can withstand the below-zero temperatures of the surface. I did that, but the effect was to cause the external skin to shrivel in a mummy-like fashion, even though I worked — with great difficulty — in a sealed chamber duplicating the conditions on the surface. It demanded a protective suit on my part, heated gloves, and so on.

'Putting it briefly, the human skin is not of the quality necessary to stand that temperature. It demands something of the cellular formation of an armadillo, and it isn't possible to create it synthetically. The man on whom I made the experiment died shortly afterwards. It then occurred to me that a woman, possessing more layers of surface flesh, might be a better subject. If I could at least make her adaptable, there might be a way of changing the sex of some of the women to male and getting around mating difficulties that way. I regret to say it failed. The woman's skin shriveled in the same way as the man's.'

Drew said nothing. There were no words he could find.

'I found afterwards, upon analysis of the cadavers, that the changing of the nervous system does other fatal things, too. It destroys all the basic emotions such as hate, fear, sex-impulse, and so on. And it also makes the control of the brain erratic. It destroys the subject completely! I'm sorry, Mr. Drew, but we're compelled to write the whole thing off.'

'It would seem,' Drew said bitterly, 'that Fate is doing her utmost to tantalise us, Doctor. As you are aware from reports from the surface, the sunspots have ceased spreading — which holds out a fair promise of a return to normal in the distant future. Yet by that time there will be nobody left to appreciate it. The 'adapted' men and women was our last hope, I'm afraid. All we older ones can do is sit around and watch for a newborn future, in which none of us can take part! If only there were some other way of bringing normal children into the world!'

'A problem beyond surgical skill,' the surgeon answered. 'Best thing we can do is pray for a miracle.'

With a cynical smile he rose, nodded, and then left the office. For some moments Drew remained thinking, holding the pipe he had ceased to smoke. He put it to his mouth, reflected, and then he turned to the radio-relay system and switched it on.

'Friends, wherever you are!' he called, and he had a mental vision of the peoples of the underworld throughout the planet pausing in their occupations to listen to him. 'Friends, I have something of great importance to tell you. It is not good news, so do not start building up hopes; but it can perhaps *become* good. The facts, simply, are these:

'On the one hand, the sunspots responsible for our retreat from the cosmic rays have ceased spreading and that means that one day they will probably decline and in the future the surface may become habitable again. On the other hand, despite every experiment, there seems to be no way of perpetuating the race so it can enjoy the day of freedom when it comes. Unless a normal child of each sex is born somewhere in this underworld we, as a race, cannot survive. That is the issue.

'Science has failed, but perhaps we have been so preoccupied with the material fundamentals we have forgotten the things spiritual in our hour of need. In the days before the Blight, drought brought forth prayers for rain from the community; just as excess rain brought prayers for fine weather. The problem here is similar. I ask all of you to pray for two normal children, one of each sex. How worthy we are to have the prayer answered I don't know, but at least let us be willing.

'To that end, I am asking all the leaders of spiritual sects to designate one particular hour to this world-wide appeal to the Power Who made us; for without the help of that Power we cannot survive.'

Here Drew stopped, trusting to the

innate decency of the people to act according to their lights. His faith was not misplaced. The sudden call to things spiritual swept like a flame through the underworld, and there was hardly one who did not respond.

For perhaps the first and last time in Earth's history, every man and woman remained with bowed head at the appointed time, praying that, if worthy, the race might survive.

Then again the threads were taken up, yet somehow with a newborn hope, a feeling of lightness, as though the crushing load of impending doom had been lifted for a while.

Drew, satisfied that he had done everything humanly possible. continued with his normal work thereafter, ruling the destinies not only of his own immediate city but those of the world, in conjunction with the governments of other buried populations. Ken, too, spent his time wrestling with the still many engineering problems connected with the city's slow development and advancement.

Observations showed that the sunspots were still stationary, neither increasing nor decreasing. The surface conditions remained unchanged, as did the intensity of cosmic rays. Crisis had been reached: the balance would now swing one way or the other — to newborn life, or utter doom.

Weeks drifted into months. The February of the following year came, with no apparent change in season, since the normal solstices had ceased to have meaning with the coming of the Blight. Then, towards the end of February, came news. It was only a registration form to commence with, but sent by express messenger to Drew's headquarters. He read it, and for a moment, his hand shook. The record showed that a male child had been born to a young man and woman in the workers' section, and that every medical test — handled by the head surgeon — had shown the child was completely normal!

Drew flashed the news to the world. There were celebrations, prayers of thanks, then more prayers in the hope that a female child would appear somewhere. In the meantime, the boy was taken over by the experts and watched closely. He was guarded and treasured more zealously than the most precious of elements, all unaware in his happy babyhood that he formed the nucleus of a race if a partner ever came into being.

If! Therein lay the first doubt of waiting humanity. They began to wonder as weeks went by and what few births occurred were those of freaks. February moved on into March, April, and at length June. Some people had even forgotten the miracle of the boy, and were cursing the fates again, quite convinced that no girl would ever appear to complete the sequence.

But it happened — and almost as though Nature were trying to recompense for the delay, twin girls were born to the wife of a laboratory technician. Again there were celebrations, and Drew in particular was profoundly thankful. Except for perhaps some of the spiritual heads, he was the only man who remembered to express his gratitude —

alone in his headquarters, with all the devoutness that he brought to his more material, everyday tasks.

To him this appeared like the hurdling of the final difficulty. With both sexes normal again, twenty years or less would see the commencement of a scientifically planned race. In the meantime, further normal children might be born. If not, it did not signify. A start could be made.

Ken was one of many who raised questions concerning the births.

'How do you account for normalcy when others were abnormal?' he asked Drew one 'evening', when they were relaxing together in one of the city's leisure-hour clubs.

'I don't.' Drew gave a shrug, his solitary hand playing with the stem of his wine glass. 'Or if I do, I have to accept the head surgeon's explanation — that the mothers of the boy and two girls are still only fifteen. To the Easterners, before the Blight, that would have been considered a desirable marrying age for a girl: we used to think differently, until we came down here and marriage and offspring became the most essential factor in our lives. Anyway, since the mothers are only fifteen, it means that they were not quite fourteen when the exodus down here was made a year ago. Cosmic radiation did not have much effect on the parental germ plasm in their case, because it was still not fully formed. That, biologically, is the surgeon's explanation. I prefer to call it a miracle.'

Ken nodded but did not pursue the subject. He was less inclined to the spiritual side than Drew. The death of Thayleen had made his outlook atheistic.

'Whatever the cause,' Drew said finally, 'the future is at last assured. Once we let the sun start recovering, and we know that the children of these children will be able to go back to the world we once knew.'

'Suppose they don't wish to? Suppose they become so accustomed to life down here that surface life proves repulsive? Just as Kasper Hauser, the galley slave, did not like the other world when released and asked to go back to slavery. Environment does queer things.'

'True,' Drew admitted. 'However, we shall scientifically create external conditions around these children in the hope they will develop the inborn strain to live on the outside of their planet.'

And at Drew's suggestion, this method was adopted. The surgeon and his associates did everything possible to bring up the three children in as near normal conditions as they could; but even they could not duplicate the fresh winds of the surface world, the brilliant sun on a sparkling sea, the gentle warmth of a summer evening . . . No matter how perfect the synthesis, nothing could match the original. Only the years could show whether the youngsters would have any inclination to leave their prison.

Drew, satisfied that the major part of his battle was over, became less furiously energetic as the months went by. With his affairs of State more or less on even keel, it was simply a matter of routine to keep things going smoothly.

Ken, too, found he had less work to do as the final engineering details of the city were finished. It even appeared that for many years to come there would be a period of relaxation.

Then to Drew came the first signs of even more disturbances in what he had believed were calm waters. The observation reports relayed to him every day referred each time to storms on the surface of a violence and duration surpassing anything that had ever been known in the electrical storms of the early days of the Blight.

So constantly did the information reach him he finally decided to investigate for himself and, as usual, Ken went with him to the surface. In proofed suits, and inside a large duplicate machine of the Johnson projectile, they left the underworld via the temporarily opened shaft, and Drew hurtled the rocket-projectile to 1,000 feet before he levelled out. Below, the shaft closed again until his radio order should have it re-opened.

Both lying flat on the transparent floor, he and Ken studied the landscape. It was powdered with frost, the hills and dales sharply clear with only thin air interven-ing. The sun, at what would normally have been high noon position, was red and sombre, three parts of the surface obscured, the spots no larger, yet no smaller.

'I don't see any signs of a storm,' Ken said at last, through the audiophone. 'Maybe the technician was seeing things.'

'Hardly! If you take a look below you'll notice that the ground looks as though it has been pounded with meteors. It's full of small-sized craters, the sort of craters small atomic explosions might make.'

Unable to understand the problem, Ken did not pursue it. He studied the view below more intently, then as the vessel flew on, he pointed through the main observation window.

'There's a storm!' he exclaimed. 'Beyond that range of hills — ' He whistled. 'And one hell of a storm, too! I never saw such lightning to equal it — and yet a clear sky! What sort of business do you call that?'

Drew slowed the projectile down, watching the distant violet blue flickering as he did so. A tremendous disturbance was in progress some thirty miles away, apparently concentrated on the ground itself, yet hurtling electrical bolts sky-wards at intervals.

'That's no storm,' Drew's sober voice commented at last. 'It's *atomic power*! Deep down in my mind I have always been afraid of this, but I'd hoped with the cessation of sunspots that it would not come to it . . . I was wrong. It means that the entire magnetic field has broken down and we are fully open to the increased level of cosmic radiation from that nearby neutron star!'

'Is that significant?' Ken asked, puzzled.

'I'll tell you when we get below.'

The gloom that had come into Drew's voice worried Ken. In his brief trip, Drew had changed from an almost light-hearted scientist into the troubled, harassed man of the early days of the Blight. Through his face-visor his serious expression was dimly visible in the tiny light from the instrument board.

He swung the projectile's nose round, gave the radio order for the shaft to be reopened, and less than thirty minutes later he and Ken were back again in the headquarters. Drew sat down heavily at his desk and pushed his empty pipe in his mouth.

'I can sum everything up in two words, Ken,' he said at last. 'We're beaten!'

'Beaten? But that's preposterous! You were saying only a little while ago that we have only to wait for the future — '

'That was before I had seen what's happening on the surface. You have got to know the truth, Ken, same as everybody else will have to. We have fought every battle so far, and won it — but this time there is no answer. Those three children on whom our hopes are pinned will never survive to see the surface, and neither shall we. In a year, even less, the whole surface of the Earth, and down to a depth of countless miles, will have vanished in cosmic dust.'

Ken felt his lips become dry.

'Up there — ' Drew jabbed his dead pipe ceilingwards. 'Up there we saw an atomic storm. That is what those other disturbances must have been. They are the ultimate catastrophe in the cosmic radiation chain. You see in cosmic rays there are protons five to ten times as powerful as those with which our physicists smash the atoms of other elements. They are raining down on Earth now, quite unshielded, the last vestige of the magnetic field having collapsed.

'Accordingly, Earth's surface is being blasted by an ever increasing series of atomic storms. Prior to the Blight this would not have been catastrophic. Normally, it is simply not possible for atomic disintegration to spread spontaneously from atom to atom. The interposition of ordinary matter acts as a 'moderator' and stifles the chain reaction. But, increasingly, the atoms forming the surface of the Earth *are no longer ordinary matter!* They are becoming highly radioactive! In addition to radiation, the surface has until very recently been bombarded by massive solar flares . . .

'The atoms of the radioactive matter are now being smashed by the heavy cosmic radiation protons, and in the process high-speed neutrons are being emitted in the tens of thousands. They in turn split up other matter — an endless chain, a devouring, fiery corrosion, eating Earth away into dust with ever increasing speed . . . '

Drew stopped for a moment, and then said:

'The chain reactions will of course peter out whenever ordinary matter intervenes. But under the constant onslaught from space, more and more tracts of the surface will become radioactive! It means that little by little the erosion will spread and eat down to where we are. As layer after layer of rock surface is exploded away by the endless chain of atomic destruction, we shall become more and more exposed to cosmic radiation again, our rock barrier becoming ever thinner. Wherever we go — down, down, even to the fringe of the nickle-iron core of Earth itself, if we could ever dig that deep, we cannot escape. There must come a time — and rapidly — when we shall be overwhelmed.'

Ken sank back in his chair, his face grey.

'You — you mean that as Earth is exploded away from above us we shall find ourselves once again with thickening skin and increasing hair? You mean that henceforth the women who have given perfect children will give freaks? We're like ants on a burning log? There's no way out?'

'None! The miracle of the children happened, but I'm afraid very few remembered to say thank you. As a race, we're a mighty selfish breed, Ken. We live only for ourselves. The sun has a chance to return to normal, and we have normal children. But, all that can happen now is that the sun may, in the future, become normal again, to shine down on the emptiness of dust where Earth once whirled. The other planets in the System will go, too.'

Drew laid his pipe in the brass ashtray and switched on the radio relay. As he had given hopeful news in the past, so he now gave the information that doomed the last warriors of the human race. Everybody knew when he had finished that within a few weeks they would be exposed to the naked fire of atomic destruction.

'To each of us there remains the privilege of facing this ultimate catastrophe with courage,' Drew finished, his voice unshaken but tinged with sadness. 'We have fought to the end, and lost. In the battle against the elemental forces of the Universe — blind, ruthless forces backed by illimitable power — puny Man must finally be the loser . . . So it is now. We once believed in God, and for a brief while we had the miracle of the children. That the miracle cannot be developed is not our fault. There is nothing we can do but resign ourselves to the power which made us.'

Drew switched off. He met the eyes of Ken across the desk. Ken was smiling faintly to himself.

'Perhaps — I'll join Thayleen,' he said. 'That will make dying worthwhile . . . '

Drew picked up his pipe and examined it.

' 'So shall this insubstantial pageant fade and leave not a wrack behind',' he murmured. 'If only Oliver Goldsmith could have seen this!'

He became silent. The pipe cracked suddenly under the convulsive grip of his fingers . . .

THE END